MANHATTAN SPIRITUAL

A Novel by
Timothy Brannan

Other Books By Timothy Brannan

Into the Elephant Grass: A Viet-Nam Fable

TEACH [Also Kindle Edition]

Adventures in Another Paradise [Also Kindle Edition]

'74: A Basketball Story [Also Kindle Edition]

<u>*Instructions for Kindle Readers & Others Who Desire a Soundtrack*</u>

Download the following musical selections to enhance the reading experience with a "sound track" of musical selections.

Play prior to beginning Part One:
"All Along the Watchtower," Bob Dylan as recorded by Jimi Hendrix.

Play with Part One, Chapter 1:
"Purple Haze," Jimi Hendrix.

Play with Part One, Chapter 2:
"Star Spangled Banner," Jimi Hendrix.

Play with Part One, Chapter 3:
"A Day in the Life," John Lennon & Paul McCartney.

"Devil with the Blue Dress On," Mitch Ryder & the Detroit Wheels.

"Norweigan Wood," John Lennon & Paul McCartney.

Play with Part One, Chapters 5 - 7:
"Give Peace a Chance," John Lennon.

Play with Part Two, Chapter 8:
"Like a Rollin' Stone," Bob Dylan.

Play with Part Two, Chapters 9 - 10:
"It's Alright, Ma . . . ." Bob Dylan.

Play with Part Two, Chapter 11 - 12:
"The Hour That The Ship Comes In," Bob Dylan.

Play with Part Two, Chapters 12 -15:
  " Prologue, August 29, 1968," Chicago.

Play with Part Two, Chapters 18 - 22:
  "Like a Rolling Stone," Bob Dylan.

Play with Part Three, Chapter 23 - 24:
  "Sympathy for the Devil," Rolling Stones.

Play with Part Three, Chapter 25:
  "Happiness is a Warm Gun," John Lennon & Paul McCartney.

Play with Part Four, Chapters 26 - 27:
  "Manhattan Spiritual," Billy Maxted.

  "Can't Find My Way Home," Blind Faith.

Play with Part Four, Chapter 33:
  "All Along the Watchtower," Bob Dylan version.

End of
Instructions for Kindle Readers & Others
Who Desire a Soundtrack

"There must be some kinda way outta here,"
said the joker to the thief
"There's too much confusion, I can't get no relief
Businessmen, they drink my wine,
Plowmen dig my earth
None of them along the line
Know what any of it is worth"

"No reason to get excited,"
The thief, he finally spoke.
"There are many here among us
Who feel that life is but a joke
But you and I, we've been through that,
And this is not our fate
So let us not talk falsely now,
The hour is getting late."

All along the watchtower,
Princes kept the view
While all the women came and went,
Barefoot servants, too

Outside in the cold distance
A wildcat did growl
Two riders were approaching, and
The wind began to howl.

"All Along the Watchtower," from John Wesley
Harding, Bob Dylan

Part One

*The way that can be named
is not the way*

Tao Te Ching

Purple haze, all in my brain;
Eyes these days, they don't see the same.
Acting funny, but I don't know why;
Excuse me while I kiss the sky.
Purple haze, all around;
Don't know if I'm coming up or down.
Ever happy or in misery;
Whatever it is, that girl put a spell on me.
Help me! Help me!
Purple haze, all in my eyes;
Don't know if it's day or night.
You got me moving, blowing my mind;
Is it tomorrow or just the end of time?

"Purple Haze," Jimi Hendrix

1

The letter came by special courier to the Quonset hut inside the perimeter patrolled by mounted Capitol Hill Police. That was where he and Kip Klopps called home in those days of confrontation. The Military Intelligence Mobile Van that acted as their base of operations was only a short walk from the Quonset hut and Tent City serving as temporary quarters for the military security forces deployed to protect the Pentagon.

OFFICE OF THE MAYOR
CITY HALL
ROANOKE PARK, N.C. 27605

October 17, 1967

SSG Matthew Parkrow
Permanent Party
Fort Holabird, Maryland

Dear Son:

I hear you've been selected as part of the security forces for when them radical hippie communists march on Washington in a few days. A real switch from those other marches you made back when you were still a kid in college. You marched with them, then. But, that was before you put away childish things. Now we're all right proud of your service, Matthew. Proud that you didn't run off to Canada or desert to Sweden or go off to federal prison like so many of your weirdo generation did. Traitors! I'm sorry, son, but I just don't understand what's happened to your generation of young men. When I was your age, The War was in full swing, and I knew what I had to do for my country. I had to help Uncle Sam kick the shit out of Hirohito and Hitler. And, believe you me we didn't hold back on our duty. We went at that fighting with a vengeance. You haven't held back either, Matthew, like so many of the shaggy bastards have. Jail or exile's too damned good for them if you ask me.

I guess you must've read by now that Roanoke Park has another four years of "Progress with Parkrow." Thanks to you, son, and all your medals, I got re-elected by a landslide. I know we've had our differences over the years, but they've been only political, not fundamental. And God's been good to us, son. If only you would come back to your senses about that and quit seeing His practical jokes in every corner. You carry around your guilt like you used to carry around that black Duke Snider bat, you know, the one with the silver lettering that I gave you for your fifteenth birthday when you made the high school team. You used to sleep with it on nights before a big game, even when you were a big deal senior.

Damn! Before you took that step forward to join the Army, the proudest day of my life was in the state championship game when you hit that grand slam against them citified fools from Raleigh with their airs and education. Except, maybe, for the day when you and Ward Crampton signed with the State University. The best damned double play combination in the whole damned state. Damn!

Alecia told me how Ward became missing in action, about you driving him to that Bien Hoa air base and all, and about seeing that he got on that helicopter on time. Listen, son, you can't carry around all that guilt inside you for something you never could have done anything about anyway. Hell, Ward Crampton might have been court martialed or worse--if there could be anything worse--if you hadn't gotten him up that fateful morning and driven him to the air base like any good buddy would've. How could you have known that he'd get shot down by a VC rocket when he was going into the Iron Triangle? Well, at least Ward is only officially missing in action. Where there's no death certificate, there's still hope, son.

Remember how all those reporters flashed pictures and questions at you all because you didn't sign with the pros like poor, dead Turkey Locklear? Some say he didn't even get a chance to cash his bonus check. The way his mother tells it, only a few days passed after he signed before he died of lymph gland cancer. Nobody even knew before that! His mother also tells me that the day after Ward's mother shot herself with the twelve gauge Henderson had given to Ward for Christmas a few years back--you remember it don't you? The one with the persimmon inlaid stock . . . a beautiful shotgun.--Anyway, the day after she blew her face off in her front yard under that American flag they always had flying--then it was at half mast for Ward--Henderson came home from a medical convention in New York with this story that a young man who could be Ward's twin was working as a waiter part time in some restaurant near Columbia University. Well, after Ida's funeral, Henderson flew straight back to New York to find out for himself. Naomi Locklear says he found that restaurant, but when he asked the owner about Ward and showed him a picture, the radical-looking bastard with a Garfinkle African hairdo said, ANo, man. He's never been in here, man. Never worked here, man." How did he know? Henderson had asked. AI memorize every face that comes through my doors, man. Even yours, man. How else would I know, man?" Henderson told Naomi that the boy was downright rude. Those Yankees got no raising. Everybody knows that.

I wanted to surprise you with that news. You'll be real interested in who Henderson got the story from. And probably very surprised! Just come home for a short visit, son, and I'll tell you where the restaurant is and who told Henderson about it.

It's been months since Alecia told me how you were "just passing through" while on leave from Vietnam before going back to Fort Holabird. She says you only stayed long enough to go to Oakwood and put petunias on your Mother's grave. It's not your fault that your Mother died when you were born, either, even though you seem to think it somehow is. You weren't any more responsible for your Mother's death than you were for Ward's.

Alecia told me that you're finally going to be a teacher, an intelligence instructor at the Army Intelligence School. But Alecia told me also that there was not a word for me. Matthew, don't shut your father out, son. After all, we're the same flesh and blood. All that's left of it is in your veins. I'll put some flowers on Estelle's grave for you and me. Next time you're home, maybe we can visit her together like we used to back in the old days. Okay?

Oh well. Did I say I'm as proud of you as I was when you hit that grand slam against the Raleigh Caps in '63? Well, son, I am! Guarding the Pentagon. Damn!

May God bless you and keep you safe from the commie radical hippie queers.

Sincerely,

Jason Parkrow
Mayor

2

Matthew Parkrow refolded the letter along already-tearing creases and stuck the six pages of stationery into his starched jungle fatigue blouse pocket. Poor man. Jason had been measuring him against that three-hundred-and-thirty-foot home run ever since he hit it. He had tried to tell his father, even then, that it was a foul ball, that the umps didn't see it or didn't call it for some reason. But Jason had given him the same song and dance that Ward had. If it had really been a foul ball, then why didn't one of the three best high school umps in the entire state of North Carolina call it?

Matthew had no answer for that question then. He didn't have an answer to that question now. But, he knew what he knew. After all, the ball was off his bat. No one else's. It was a foul ball. Not that he complained all that much about it. After all, that grand slam had made him the big hero of the year. It had helped land him a grant-in-aid to State. More importantly, though, it had been an invaluable lesson in life. A koan regarding actuality as opposed to reality. The grand slam had actually been a foul ball. But, as the result of a missed call, it became, in reality, the game winning home run for the state baseball championship.

He glanced at the date on his Seiko watch: OCT 21. "How the hell did Jason know four days ago who the security personnel for the Washington anti-war march would be?" he muttered. That had been "Eyes Only" Top Secret shit! He remembered what his roommate Kip Klopps had said earlier when he'd asked him the same question. "It's a club thing, man. You know, all those hot shot elected officials are in it. The Tri-Lateral Commission or some such shit. They tell each other everything, you know?"

In his periphery, Matthew spotted Colonel Otis Flanger striding past the row of jeeps, troop transport trucks (cattle cars to GI's), and operations vans along the ridge. His crisp cadence carried him toward their special MI mobile van with a sense of purpose reserved only for those men who, like Jason, approached everything in a self-righteous vacuum. Matthew, Specialist Five Donaldson, and Buck Sergeant Kip Klopps manned Colonel Flanger's intelligence van and comprised his primary instructor cadre. The van was Flanger's pride and passion, the training innovation he'd been working for. On the scene practice. An on the scene model for students.

Flanger had been touring troops through since six hundred hours yesterday morning. They were from the school at Fort Holabird where Matthew and the other van personnel were instructors, so he knew most of them. At least, he knew their faces. He even taught some of them in his present "Order of Battle" and "Surreptitious Entry and Surveillance" courses. Eddie Donaldson instructed classes in materials classification and handling of classified materials, and Kip taught imagery interpretation.

Each was a citizen soldier filling in the last days on his "Short Timer's Calendar" in magic marker and grease pencil colors. Matthew colored in days sixty-four and sixty-five with a blue grease pencil on his photocopy of the calendar which he had duct-taped to the inside front cover of his olive drab notebook. There he stored his lesson plans, lecture notes, and his personal diary entries and comments.

Damn! He might actually have a lead on Ward after all this time. But, it was through Jason. Did he really want to go back to Jason's house only to find out about what was probably just another wild goose chase? Could he abide his father's rattle, prattle, and chattel?

With the same grease pencil, he entered the Julian date 67294 into the Daily Log and marked a big blue X at the Washington Monument where--according to the latest aerial reconnaissance photos and intelligence summaries--

12

the tribe had ostensibly gathered for today's march on the Pentagon.

The last time they had gathered like this was in sixty-five for the "I have a dream" march. He'd been a senior at State University then. An ex All-American second baseman after he quit the team to become one of the tribe. Not one of the pigs like now. He'd given up his grant-in-aid in protest of a war he later fought. He still did not have an answer to the basic question his actions had begged: Is it better to be a Socrates unsatisfied or a pig satisfied? Because, part of him was still out there with them, even now. Yet, he also knew that he was already so short that he needed a hand up to get over the threshold of their Quonset hut door each morning. He only had thirty-five days left. Short!

"Great infra-reds!" Klopps chuckled as he attempted to hand some photos directly to Matthew and by-pass Donaldson's tight-assed classification syndrome.

Donaldson snatched the blurred shots of heat mass before Matthew could reach them. He slapped them onto his desk, protecting them from Klopps and Parkrow with hunched shoulders turned away from their only potential avenue of attack--from behind his desk and to his left. Like a dog sniffing out a place to piss, Donaldson perused the infrared photographs, first under various magnifying glasses, then under a stereoscope. "These are, most definitely, shots of the gathering storm. These must be classified SECRET!"

"Christ, Donaldson!" Klopps stomped back toward his desk and developing lab in the dark rear corner of the van, shaking his skinned blond head and muttering loud enough for anyone to hear. "On what fucking basis, Donaldson? On what fucking basis, man?"

"Kiiip! Come on, now. These photos deal with enemy troop movements. Regulations require that they be classified accordingly."

"They're pictures of fucking heat masses rising from the fucking pavement, for Christ sake!" Klopps howled from his dark corner. "If that's the 'gathering storm', Donaldson, I'll kiss your fucking ass. And, believe me, man, I don't want to kiss your fat ass."

Colonel Flanger's spit shined boots hit the first metal step at the van door. "Ten hut!" Matthew bellowed out the command like his Drill Sergeant in basic training used to do it and probably still did. Flanger was pretty gung-ho about that kind of shit. He liked loud commands, snappy salutes, and starched, pressed fatigues. So give them to him for the next thirty-five days and counting. Why not? Short!

"Good morning, gentlemen." He popped a limp-wrist salute toward Matthew, his senior NCO, as he crossed the threshold. He was right proud of Staff Sergeant Parkrow. Almost like the son he'd lost in Nam.

Matthew's salute was crisp and not the least bit limp-wrist. He noted with some humor that the Colonel didn't seem to need any help getting over the threshold. He sure as hell wasn't short. He was in for life. Matthew fought back a chuckle. "Good morning, Colonel Flanger, sir!" Must maintain decorum, act out the scene according to the rules and regulations, even classifying Donaldson's photos of heat waves if that was what it took. Play the role scripted for him even if it didn't suit him. Only thirty-five days left. Short!

"Good morning, sir," Donaldson muttered.

In the shadows of his corner, Klopps nodded, then turned back to his developing pans to process the last of the early morning shots just delivered by special courier only minutes before from their photo recon unit.

"Continue to march, men." Flanger fumbled in his fatigue pockets for a match to light the cheroot he perpetually chewed from the right side of his mouth. As he found matches and lit the cigar, he continued. "Don't let me get in the way of operations here, Staff Sergeant. I'm just checking things out before bringing through the next batch of students for a tour." He swaggered around the fifteen-by-twenty-five-foot confines of the van, peeking at photographs hanging from clothes pins on a piece of line strung across the lighter corner near the door. He poked through messages and intelligence reports, shuffled papers on Donaldson's desk. Klopps followed him at a safe three pace distance, whispering something to the Colonel which actually made him cackle. Flanger turned back toward the front of the van where Matthew stood at ease. "Staff Sergeant Parkrow. I want to compliment you and your men for the way you've handled these tours." He paused, and the silence could have been spelled "b u t."

"Thank you, sir."

He motioned to Matthew. "Can you come back here for a moment?"

"Yes, sir." Matthew skirted Donaldson's inquiry-twisted face and his swivel chair--the only one in the van. He clomped over the metal floor to the dark room corner where Klopps and Flanger stood hunched over each other at Kip's desk. They whispered and chuckled like a couple of school kids while they waited for something to finish in the final wash pan. It was time's like these when Matthew wished that he'd extended in Viet-Nam--bad as it was at times--forever, if necessary. He just couldn't get into the stateside Army life, the spit-and-polish bullshit, the gawks from his civilian peers on the streets when he walked by in his uniform and his Flanger-required sidewall haircut. He was their enemy, now, just because he wore the Army green and short hair. Soon, he hoped, they would learn how many brothers were in the military just like himself.

"Sir?" Matthew leaned down, glancing over their shoulders at the clarifying photograph in the tray. A copy of one of the infra-reds that Donaldson wanted to classify SECRET. Flanger pointed to the slick paper with its heat zones becoming more visible as the seconds plodded. "This is what Donaldson wants to classify SECRET?" As he whispered his question, smoke from his cheroot puffed from the corners of his mouth like steam from under a locomotive in an Arthur Penn western.

Matthew attempted to hold back the mounting laughter, but he couldn't hide the giggles in his eyes as they both glanced around at Donaldson. "Yes, sir. I'm afraid so, sir. Night infra-red heat mass shots of traffic passing the Washington Monument, sir."

"Is that how you read them, Sergeant Klopps?"

"Obviously so, sir? I've got kids in my class who wouldn't fuck that up, sir."

"Are you sure, Staff Sergeant Parkrow, that this character's actually experienced?" Flanger's mouth continued to bellow smoke as he talked.

"Well, sir. His Military 201 File says that he trained at Holabird in sixty-six. That's the same year that Sergeant Klopps and myself trained there. He spent a tour in the Nam, Colonel, as an imagery interpreter for some MI unit out of Nha Trang."

"Did either of you . . . ." Flanger's beady black eyes darted back and forth, conspiratorially, from Matthew to Kip. "Did either of you know this character, Donaldson, before? At Holabird? In Nam?"

They both shook their heads.

"So it seems he just appeared out of nowhere." Flanger's eyes rolled in their oversized sockets as his thin blue lips chewed the cheroot that had gone out as usual after a few puffs. "Then, for all we know, my information that he's CID or something like that, could very well prove correct? His 201 file might well be a complete and clever fiction."

Klopps eyed his NCO-in-charge and his closest friend in the Army world. "I don't know, sir. What do you think, Matthew, ah, Staff Sergeant Parkrow?"

Matthew shrugged. "Beats me, sir." He wasn't going to get involved unnecessarily in Flanger's military-bound paranoia about being spied upon from within constantly.

He knew that MI planted spies in the local bars on Holabird Avenue and Dundalk Avenue as well as on "The Block" to keep eyes and ears out for young recruits suffering from diarrhea of the mouth. So, it wouldn't be any surprise at all if everyone in the fucking van except for him was CID or CIA or GKW (God-Knows-What). Probably, even Kip. But. If you can't take a joke, fuck it! Thirty-five days until it all ends.

"I wonder." Flanger draped his starched jungle fatigue bloused arms over their shoulders. "I wonder if there is some way to, ah, shall we say get him to transfer out of Fort Holabird?" He coughed around his cheroot stub. "Just as a precautionary measure, of course."

"All I know, sir, is that if he is undercover like your sources say, then he isn't going anywhere very easily."

"Well, I must tell you, gentlemen, that he has been the only black mark on our van tours. The students don't seem to like him for some reason. They think he's dinky dao." Otis Flanger thumped the residue of cigar ashes into the classified burn can under the plywood counter which held Kip's developing trays as if for emphasis. "And, that, alone, makes him a big threat to me and to my plans. Not even counting if he really is CID or whatever."

"Maybe he'll defect to the hippies, sir."

"Christ, Kip!" Matthew could no longer resist. "Don't hold your fucking breath! Donaldson's the most reactionary fucker I ever knew. He'd never do anything like that, especially if he really is an agent sent to spy on the Colonel."

Flanger smirked. "That's not a bad idea, though, Sergeant Klopps." He glanced over his left shoulder at Donaldson huddled over his desk rearranging the piles of reports, messages, photographs, maps, hand scribbled notes from Parkrow, Klopps, and officials inside the Pentagon down and off to their left. "Not bad at all."

The sun was just seeping through the door. Another brittle October morning snapped to life, languid as the

17

Colonel's strides out of the dark corner of the van toward the light, his arms still wrapped around Klopps and Parkrow pulling them along with him. Matthew's eyes followed the Colonel, finally resting on Donaldson's red flat-top glazed with pomade he'd obviously hoarded from the fifties. It sparkled in a shaft of the sunlight now streaming through the door while he continued to shuffle through documents on his desk as though he were really busy instead of classifying nothing as he strained to hear their whispered conversation.

"If we could pull this off, gentlemen, well . . . ." He stifled what appeared to have almost been a shriek of glee. He turned toward Klopps, grinning, and released them both from the grip of his arms. Then, he motioned for Matthew to follow him outside.

Poor Donaldson, poor stupid bastard. Matthew shook his head as he followed Flanger to the van door and the sunrise, remembering the day that Brian Epstein died and their own private wake in Baltimore.

3

"Woke up; fell out of bed; dragged a comb across my head." The words of "Day in the Life" slipped through smoke and odors of beer and Philly steak sandwiches smothered in grilled onions toward laminated plastic tables in the dim back room off of the main bar at the Holabird Inn. It was the only part of the traditional hang-out across from the main gate of Fort Holabird where battleship gray and OD green buildings couldn't stare at them as they sucked up their suds and slugged down their shots.

"Jesus, Donaldson!" Kip Klopps wagged his toe-head, then tossed off the dregs of his shot of vodka. He smacked his lips and sipped now tepid water as a chaser. It had been sitting there as long as they had. Since breakfast. They had broken their fast this morning with Bloody Mary's and screwdrivers over easy. "You mean to tell me that you still think we're all being spied on by the communists?" he smirked.

Matthew slumped on his elbows over his shot of Jack Daniels green label and the remaining half of an Iron City beer. He glared at the dancing red-white-and-blue spots in the Budweiser sign hanging from the pine paneled wall behind Donaldson who slugged down the last of his Schmidts beer like it was the very last of the Schmidts in all of Baltimore and perhaps all of the east coast. Matthew felt outside of himself like he was on acid, as if he were perched on the glittering sign watching them around the table. He felt like he had when he first came back from the Nam, like they all had, he guessed. He had felt a lot of distance.

"Fuck, Donaldson!" Klopps continued. "When I got my orders to this place from basic training out of Fort Jackson--you know, Tent City--nobody down there even knew where Fort Holabird was much less what it was. My Captain told me that I was the only man in the whole fucking training division to get orders to this place." He paused. "In a whole fucking training division, Donaldson. Do you begin to get the picture here?"

Matthew sloshed down the shot of sour mash. His body shuddered. He didn't bother with the beer chaser. He had given up on that shortly after lunch--a Mai Tai and all the pretzels he could wolf down. Besides, he liked the afterburn in his throat and stomach, especially on a night like this one when the rain drenching the Dundalk area stung like sleet. Best anti-freeze known to man. "Shit," he heard his numbing lips spit at Donaldson. "Shit. Kip's right. Even the man who sold me my ticket on the train from Roanoke Park had trouble finding it on his fare sheets." Matthew burped from deep inside his abdomen. "He wasn't even sure where it was after he had sold me the ticket, for Christ sake. 'All I know is the train stops at Baltimore, Maryland,' he had whined. It echoed all over that old train station."

"Only a select few cabbies in Baltimore even knew that the fort was about three miles from the train station. So, how the hell are the commies going to know?" Kip snatched Matthew's beer and gulped it. His face contorted. "Ugh!" He gyrated his head, rolling his slate eyes, and shoved the glass back at Matthew. "You can bet your ass, my good man, that your fucking beer, here, is about as palatable as Donaldson's fucking paranoia."

Matthew felt his lips curling in a mock sneer. "I guess that'd be like betting my ass against the Green Bay Packers, huh?"

"Yeah!"

"Okay. Okay!" Donaldson's meaty fingers tore at the smoke above their heads. "You don't believe me? Watch this!" He glared at Matthew and Kip. "Nurse! Help, nurse!" His hazel eyes dulled by beer and fumes that, at times, seem to be absorbing them instead of the other way around. "Soooo, you don' believe me, huh? Don' believe old Eagle-ears Donaldson, huh? Nurse!"

20

The blond toothpick, Dana, finally shuffled across the scuffed linoleum floor toward their table. It was her fate not only to look like Twiggy but to also have their table for the evening. "Watch this, goddamn it," Donaldson spluttered again. Dana bent beside him, touching his shoulders and pocked neck with her handsful of heaven held in place loosely by a scant blue halter. "'Nother round here, Dana, if you please."

"Sure, Eddie, honey." She winked a blue eye at Kip and Matthew as she purred in Donaldson's pixie ear. They were her regulars. Eddie was an occasional tag-along. "Anything else you want, Eddie, honey?" She allowed her breasts to move just slightly along his shoulder.

Doanaldson's face flushed lavender in the iridescent lights filtering through the smoke. "W . . . what would you take for a Dana sandwich on clean sheets?" The baby fat that still clung to his jowls seemed to vibrate as he continued to redden and giggle.

Dana jerked up. "Why, I'm just plain insulted, Eddie Donaldson." Her scarecrow arms askew, her gaunt, child face portrayed shock. She adjusted her halter to show him more breast tops and hooked her thumbs in the belt loops of her bellbottom jeans.

"Mitch Ryder and the Detroit Wheels said it best," Kip gurgled. He ruffled Donaldson's flat top. "Oh, fuck," he muttered, wiping the pomade on Donaldson's own charcoal wool slacks.

"Yeah!" Matthew seemed to be returning to his body after that last shot had settled his stomach and his head. As he leaned toward Donaldson, both he and Kip bellowed in ragged harmony: "Fe, fe, fi, fi, fo, fo, fum. Looking mighty nice, here she comes . . . . Devil with the blue dress, blue dress, blue dress. Devil with the blue dress on. Ah, devil with the . . . ah . . . blue . . . ah . ...*jeans* on."

"Well," Dana sighed against Donaldson's flabby cheek, affecting a Russian accent. "If you inzist on paying'k me, darling'k, maybe you can let'z me read one of your lit-tle

21

training'k books or zomezhing'k. I'm juzt fazinated wid'z military men and zhings." She touched his chest hair curling up under his neck between the open collar of his powder blue Gant shirt left over from Jasper State College fraternity days. "But, really, I juzt vant to know more about you, honey." She grinned, winked again at the other two. "And your vork." Turning on the heels of her boots that were made for walking, she stomped back across the floor to the doorway, glancing over her shoulder once quickly as she disappeared through the opening into the main bar room.

"See!" Donaldson's red hair glistened. It seemed to collect smoke making it look almost silver. "I told you. See, I told you!"

"I read the news today, oh boy . . . ."

"No more!" Kip raised his hands in front of his face, then covered his ears. "Please, now Dana's a spy? Please, no more of this communist spy shit at the wake," he mumbled.

"Wake? What wake?"

"Jesus H., Donaldson. Where've you been all day?"

"In the midst of paranoia," Kip choked out between convulsions. He took another short hit of Matthew's stale beer. "Phew!"

"But, paranoia's okay, Eddie. It's a Nam disease. We all suffer from it, poor devils that we are. Some just seem to suffer from it more severely than others." Matthew also tasted the beer, with caution, rolled the swallow around in his mouth, smiling. "Warm is how the Aussies drink it, too. No wonder they call it piss."

"But?" Donaldson bleared through the smoky haze at, first, Matthew and, then, Kip, his face truly blank. "What wake?"

"We'll fill you in on everything. Again." Kip did not know or understand why Donaldson seemed to have them both trapped the way he did. But, he did know it, somehow, had something to do with that night a few

22

months ago when they were stumbling from the trusty Inn. A yellow and tan lop-eared tom cat came up to Eddie and began rubbing against his leg and all and purring like the cat was in heat or something. Of course, they knew tom cats couldn't be in heat. They were only capable, like he and Matthew and, perhaps even Eddie, of being perpetually horny. As they stumbled into the treacherous boundaries of Holabird Avenue, the cat tried to follow. Eddie kept shooing him back to the curbing. Once they were safely on the fort side of the Avenue, they reeled off toward the front gate. The tom cat meowed and lurched into the street after them.

"Go back, Tom Cat!" Eddie had gurgled. "Go back!" He flailed his baby-fat arms at the cat in the road.

The cat eluded a Ford pick-up, then a Honda 175 motorbike. "Go back, goddamn it!"

Brakes squalled. A fifty-nine Buick with save the animals stickers all over it burned rubber for fifty feet or more to no avail. Thunk. Tom Cat's skull cracked like a coconut on the bumper of the Buick.

"Why didn't you go back?" Eddie wailed, his alcohol-dulled eyes transfixed on the spot where the cat jerked like a marionette controlled by a spasming hand. "Go back, please." He slumped to his knees on the concrete sidewalk, bawling. "Please."

"Nurse!" Matthew slumped back in his chair almost knocking it over as he moaned. "Nurse. Help! I'm returning to my body, and I'm soooo thirsty. Perched on that Bud sign over there, I didn't know what it was to be truly thirsty. But, I sure as hell know now that I'm back sitting in this fucking chair where thirst is a veritable way of life much like the Tao."

When Dana brought more drinks, she made change for Donaldson's ten in saran wrap silence until Matthew shoved four quarters across the table at her. "Play more songs for Brian Epstein, okay, Dana?"

"Sure, Matthew." She half-smiled.

"Whostein?"

"Epstein. Donaldson. Brian Epstein."

"We're having a wake for a Jew?"

"Yeah." Matthew tossed off half of his double Jack Daniels, blew through pursed lips which he smacked as he poured his new frosted glass full of chilled Iron City. "It's called a jakewee by us Micks."

Kip was nearly in tears he was laughing so hard.

"Next round's on the house, Matthew. Want me to go on and bring them now?"

"Sure, Dana. I, for one, am going to need it simply to get by." Matthew stumbled to his feet, pushed his plaid shirt tail back into his jeans, whistling along with the juke box: "With a little help from my friends." As he reeled passed Donaldson, he clawed at his beefy shoulder for support. Unwillingly, Matthew sunk his fingers into the thick folds of fat surrounding Eddie's shoulder blade. "It's a wake ritual. Drink. Piss. Drink. Piss. Drink, piss, drink." He lunged toward the back corner of the room, passed the Budweiser sign still blinking red, blue, and white on the shellacked wall. "Brian Epstein's car hadn't moved all weekend. That was how suspicions were first aroused that he might be dead," Matthew hurled back at Donaldson over his shoulder.

This door handle doesn't pull. "Remember. Drink. Piss. Drink." He hurled the words over his shoulder at Donaldson like grenades. This door knob must not've moved all day long either. Poor, neglected bathroom door. It cannot be what it is unless we use it. "And, Donaldson. And, occasionally, drink, piss, sing!" Come on, Matthew. You're not cracking a safe in front of twenty students now. You're just opening the fucking latrine door. He grasped the brass knob with both hand. Ah ha! He turned it counterclockwise. The knob turns!

"If you'll just open up this once, I promise to make more use of you later on." The door rattled as he continued to push and pull. "I will no longer ignore you. I swear it!"

24

He accidentally turned the knob the other way. The door flung open, bumping him against the wall. When he was in Viet-Nam, he used to judge his night out as a good one only when he had whitewash stains on his shoulders from bouncing off his hotel walls while stumbling up the stairs to the third floor and his lumpy bed.

"Thank you, god of latrine doors. Thank you," he muttered as he stumbled to the urinal beside the single stall, unzipped his fly, pulled out his aching penis, and flung his hands above his head against the scrubbed black wall tiles. His head dangled over the porcelain urinal.

"I read the news today, oh boy . . . ."

He shuddered with relief as he flooded the clear water with dark yellow urine. "Ah, first piss of the day!" Still had breakfast's Bloody Mary's stacked up for their exits like airplanes for landing at la Guardia, O'Hare, or Friendship. If I don't get completely fucked up sick this day, then I guess I never will.

"Isn't it good, Norwegian Wood?" His voice gurgled along with the faint music of a new tune on the juke box beyond the bathroom door. He mumbled phrases and mixed lyrics as though they were all part of one song. And, perhaps, in a sense they were. Christ, he couldn't get it up even if dandy Dana sat on his naked lap, nude. On his nude lap, naked. Matthew shoved himself away from the black wall, watching his reflection totter on its tennis shoes for a moment. Whew! Maybe they would have to carry him across the street tonight and sneak him passed the gate guard by holding him by the back of his jeans for a change. He probably could give a shit less, but it was one way to pass the time.

* * * * *

"So, the Beatles went to Bangor in Wales to this TM meeting with Maharishi . . . ."

"TM?" Donaldson seemed more confused than ever as Matthew wobbled back to the table and slumped into his chair.

"Transcendental Meditation. Living in the material world and all that shit, you know?" Kip's face was flushing from the effort of attempting to explain this day, again, to Donaldson. He polished off the last half of his vodka and fished out a piece of ice from his water glass, sucking on it as he continued. "Anyway, the next day, while they were at the TM meeting. Brian Epstein--their manager--was found dead in his bedroom."

Matthew rubbed his bloodshot eyes to create tears. "Not since Buddy Holly, Richie Vallens, and the Big Bopper died in a plane crash has there been such a tragedy in the music world." He stood, supporting his weight on the chair. Raising his shot glass above his head and nodding to the WAC personnel sergeant and Corporal Rossiter from supply, the first to invade the private domain of the MI enlisted men. "To Brian Epstein. May he live forever in Paul MacCartneystein, George Harrisonstein, John Lennonstein, and Richard Starkeystein. Fuck it!" He burped from deep in his stomach. "To Jews in general!"

Kip slugged down half of Donaldson's Schmidts while Donaldson passed out as he sucked in a deep gulp of smoky air as if he were about to say something. Matthew downed the rest of his double and swizzled a mouthful of beer through his teeth before he swallowed it and flopped back into his chair. "Nurse! Help! One DOA. Two barely snorting!"

4

"Yes. Donaldson defecting to the hippies. Heh? Klopps' idea rings with just the right amount of irony to suit me, Staff Sergeant." Flanger grinned around his still unlit cheroot into the sun rising out of the Potomac like a huge florescent tomato beyond the hundreds of acres of lawns and terraces that stretched about the world's largest office building--a moat of vegetation separating the Department of Defense from the web of super highways weaving from Virginia into the capital.

"It wasn't an idea, sir. It was a sarcasm."

"No matter, Staff Sergeant. No matter."

The sun beat through white clouds, showering golden light on the manicured oak and cherry trees which clustered on the hills behind the lines of OD green vans, jeeps, and quarter-ton and duce-and-a-half trucks with olive drab people scuffling in and out of them. Some of the olive shades carried M16's slung across their backs. Others, forty-fives strapped on their hips like Matthew and Colonel Flanger as they leaned their shoulders against the MI-Mobile van and whispered above the steady drone of diesel generators.

"The real concern, Staff Sergeant, is not with how to classify Klopps' comment but rather with how we set up this 'sarcasm'--if you wish--as if it had been meant as an idea."

Matthew fidgeted with the bill of his OD green baseball cap even though it already sat as squarely on his knotty head as the creases from the forceps would allow. He was scaring himself by realizing that he actually understood the gibberish Flanger had just flung at him. "Well, Colonel, if you're really serious about this, ah, there are strategies that could be employed."

"Well, then, Staff Sergeant." He nearly swallowed the stump of his cigar as he attempted to chew and yell at the same time. "Out with it! What's the big secret?"

"No big secret, sir. Just something I learned early on in 'spook' work."

"And, that is?"

"Okay. Even if he's an agent sent here to spy on you for some reason, you're still his CO. He has to obey your orders. So. Maybe. Let's see. Maybe, you could have him defect to the demonstrators under the pretext of infiltrating the enemy for you and providing you with inside intelligence. You know, sort of an undercover type assignment. Once he deserts, you disavow him and bust him for desertion."

"And you used to get paid to think up shit like that?"

Matthew could not avoid a smirk. "Beats the hell out of most any other duty I ever heard of in the Nam, sir."

"And, Donaldson would buy into this, you think?"

"I think." Matthew removed his baseball cap with the camouflage Staff Sergeant stripes tacked on its front and wiped his damp forehead with his starched fatigue sleeve. "For sure, sir. For sure. He'll go for it, sir."

"It all sounds so easy."

"It is, sir."

"Maybe too easy?"

"Someday, sir, we'll find out that memory is probably more about what we're told than about what we actually experienced."

"What the hell does that mean, Staff Sergeant?"

"Well, sir, it goes directly to your point of this maybe being too easy."

"Parkrow! Sergeant Parkrow! Come here, quick! Things are starting to pop!" blasted from the confines of the van in Eddie Donaldson's pinched voice.

Matthew looked at Flanger and shrugged toward the whining voice.

"I think that I see what you mean, Staff Sergeant." Flanger wagged his head, chuckling to himself. "Tell Donaldson," he mumbled around chuckles, "That this mission is a small but significant part of Operation

CHAOS. He'll be 'under cover' and *in communicado.* Understood, Staff Sergeant Parkrow?"

Matthew replaced his cap and snapped off a quick salute as he turned to mount the steel steps back into the van. "Understood, sir. Nice touch, sir. He'll really get off on that, for sure, sir."

"See that he does, Staff Sergeant!" Flanger guffawed, turned on his heel in a perfectly executed 'about face' and stomped off toward the, now, nearly luminous horizon mumbling to himself as he walked. "See that he does. General Latch will be very pleased. That character's becoming a real danger to our operations with his wild notions. My God, he even reported spies in the EM Club and said that some waitress at the Holabird Inn made advances toward him to elicit classified information. He's a fucking lunatic!"

Matthew watched the Colonel's back jerk from side to side as he marched exaggeratedly toward the CP van. The MI-Mobile van door's own luminescence nearly blinded him as he stumbled on the top step, wedging his right boot between the step and the stoop. "Goddamn it!"

"What's wrong, Sergeant Parkrow?" Donaldson clucked at Matthew as he fell through the doorway after jerking his boot free.

"I've got falling sickness, for Christ sake, Eddie!" Matthew leered at Donaldson as his hands hit the metal floor, absorbing the shock of the fall and keeping his uniform off the floor. "Like paranoia, it's also a Nam disease." He'd had the uniform washed and starched and pressed at the civilian laundry on Dundalk Avenue, just so he'd look STRAK, as an airborne trooper should. Heavily starched, all the creases were sharp and straight, not bent or off-angle the way they often returned from the post laundry, and he had to spread the legs of his trousers and the sleeves of his blouse with his fingers. He was, however, often puzzled over the oxymoronic implications of starched jungle fatigues.

As he shoved himself up on momentarily gimpy legs, he glanced at his name patch over his left pocket. Just above it, cloth replicas of his Airborne Ranger Wings and Combat Infantry Badge. Below, the weight of other cloth decoration replicas puckered the pocket. From bottom left to top right--the military convention of least to most importance--Good Conduct Medal, ' Viet-Nam Service Medal, Vietnamese Commendation Medal, Purple Heart, Air Medal with two oak leaf clusters, Vietnamese Cross of Gallantry, Army Commendation Medal with V device, Bronze Star with V device and two oak leaf clusters, and Silver Star. Matthew brushed off invisible dust. "A veritable Audie fucking Murphy," he smirked to himself. "I just can't walk. That's all. You know, like you get after two Schmidts." He tip toed to Donaldson's desk and peered over his shoulder. "Okay, Eddie. What you got?"

"The insurgents are on Independence Avenue Bridge."

"Insurgents?"

"Yes. Insurgents!" Donaldson beat his fists on the metal desk. "Someone's been sleeeeping!"

"No sweat, Donaldson." Matthew perused the message in Eddie's scrawl, searching for the name of the source. "We'll just have this, ah . . . ." He finally found the name scrawled at the bottom of the Intelligence Summary. "We'll have this Spec Four Jeffers court martialed. That's all there is to it!"

"Yeah, that'll teach him to report faulty intelligence."

"Hell, yes. That'll teach the fuck!"

"Cool it, Kip. Leave old Eagle-Ears alone, now. It's not his fault, after all, that Jeffers is so slow." Matthew clapped Eddie Donaldson on the back much too hard. "But, old Eddie's going to show us how it's done. He's going to be our man in the demonstration, aren't you, Eddie?"

"Mmmeee. Wwwhat dddooo yyyou mmmean?"

"You've never heard of the stammerer as hero?"

"Nnnooo."

30

"We'll fill you in later."

"You mean, like at the wake?"

"Yeah, just like at the wake."

"Meanwhile," Klopps chirped, quickly picking up on Matthew's game. "You're it!"

"Wwwhat?"

"The stammerer as hero." Kip quickly folded a photograph into an airplane. "You know, like LLLindbbberg cccrossing the AAAtlllantic." He sailed the craft at Donaldson's head.

"Like AAAmelia EEEaarhart PPPutnam."

"And MMMax CCConrad."

"Huh . . . ah . . . ."

"And, don't forget JJJohn GGGlen."

"CCChuck GGGrissom and EEEd WWWhite."

"BOOM!"

"Wwwhat?"

Matthew wrapped his arm around Donaldson's twitching beef shoulders. "See, Eddie," he whispered in his ear. The Colonel's just been notified that the, ah, insurgents are going to try and get our troops to quit their posts, to defect, to join the demonstration."

"Yeah? So?" His dirty hazel eyes bulged from tiny sockets.

"Well, you're going to do just that."

"Wwwhat?"

"Pretend to join the demonstration. Your assignment will be to infiltrate the insurgents as part of Operation CHAOS. See?"

"N . . . n . . . no."

"Look, man. This is your big chance. The Colonel asked specifically for you to handle this job." Matthew hugged Donaldson's shoulders even tighter. "You'll be able to feed us inside information on what's going down out there among the tribe. Right?" He shook Donaldson's body as he talked. "Instead of analyzing pictures, you'll be a part of them."

31

"Ohhh?" His baby fat jowls seemed to tighten with purpose as he pushed Matthew's arm from his squaring shoulders. He straightened in his swivel chair and cleared his throat. "Imagine? Me, a real live spy?" He rattled the floor beneath his chair with his boot heels as he jumped up and down, squealing in harmony with the echoing metal. "Imagine. Me. James Bond!"

5

"Hell no, we won't go! Hell no, we won't go! Hell no, we won't go!"

Their words rumbled across the horizon long before the first marchers actually crested the northern terraces. The early sun dripped over them like liquid fire.

Begana. Kelud. Awu. Bulusan. Redoubt. The swelling mass of people was like a lava flow from volcanoes with names like those, scorching the corduroy lawns with sandals, boots, bare feet. Chants and songs were their eruptions.

"All we are saying is give peace a chance . . . ."

Mount Baker still steamed in Washington, while D.C. was becoming another Izalco. Cordons of troops stretched like firebreaks between the dull stone of the Pentagon and the flowing thunder of megaphone-amplified chants and songs. "The mountain comes to Pompeii," Matthew sniggered as he leaned against the van, smoking. Would it take another two thousand years to excavate them? Who would dust away their sleep like tons of ashes?

"The insurgents should be coming over the hill pretty soon now!" Donaldson's words were garbled by the metal walls of the van.

"Huh?" Matthew cocked his ear more toward the van walls. "Say again, Donaldson."

"I said, 'the insurgents should be coming over the hill soon.'"

"Christ, Eddie! They're already over the hill. Tell Kip."

"Oh, yeah?"

Klopps clattered across the van, piled through the doorway into the copper morning. He swung over the iron railing on the left side of the steps onto the grass. "Wow, look at all those people." His eyes were slits in the sunlight. He tried to shade them with cupped hands under the bill of his cap in order to gain a clearer view of the marchers. "We should be out there, man, you know. Not here."

"In sixty-five, it was 'We shall overcome,' and we didn't. Martin Luther King had a dream, but that dream was damned to nightmare in Watts, Harlem, Newark, Detroit." Matthew pinched the fire off his cigarette and stomped it out in the damp grass with the heel of his jungle boot. He field stripped the butt from the filter and stuffed the stained tip into his right blouse pocket.

"I don't know about you, Kip, but I've been out there." He hocked and lofted an oyster through the crisp air like he and Ward Crampton used to through the musty air in the baseball locker room to see who'd come closest to hitting a urinal. Now, Ward was only the best friend of his memories, probably lofting hockers at urinals in heaven or somewhere.

Or, was he? Jason's letter certainly opened up the possibility that Ward had somehow survived the fireball of that chopper crash. Maybe, he had amnesia or something. The sighting had been confirmed, anyway, by Ward's own father.

"People just get blown away out there, Kip. Shit! Look at what those Klansmen did to the freedom riders in Mississippi. Murdered three. Buried them, symbolically, near Philadelphia."

"But, they got their's yesterday, didn't they?" Kip grabbed Matthew's left sleeve with agitated fingers, almost pulling him off balance. "Didn't you read the paper or see it on TV?"

"Yes, I saw it on last night's news at the motel." He toed the grass with his boot as if he were in the batter's box. "Seven out of twenty-one convicted. Not convicted of murder, mind you, but of violating the murder victims fucking civil rights, for Christ sake! Isn't that what the report said? Shit. Might as well call it the one-third's compromise of nineteen hundred and sixty-seven. Right?"

"Jesus, you're one cynical fucker. I never saw nobody so cynical, at least not since Sergeant Major O'Tool. Remember him? Ordinance at Long Binh?"

"Have I gotten that bad?"

"At least, Matthew. At least."

"Christ, he used to bet on how many mortar rounds Charlie would lay in on his own ammo dump." Matthew wiped his damp forehead with his sleeve. "And, he'd win, too."

"Not just once in awhile but every fucking time."

"Hell, yes. He'd bet the Cherry Boys just off the planes over at 90th Replacement Company."

Matthew wagged his head. "I bet him once."

"You didn't?"

"I did." He glanced at the white gold Seiko on his left wrist: OCT 21 10:30. "Keep me informed, Kip. I'm going to check out the cordon lines."

"Whatever you say, Sarge. But what about Donaldson's little mission? Doesn't he have to report to Flanger at the CP for his official marching orders?"

"No. He can't do that! No plausible deniability in that. Just tell him to be prepared to infiltrate at my signal. I'm his control for this mission, not Colonel Flanger. Okay?"

"Okay, Sarge. I understand."

"I don't know what my signal will be yet, but it will be unmistakable. I can promise James Bond that much." With his right fist, Matthew playfully jabbed Kip on the shoulder in the center of his Big Red One combat patch. "We'll get him into the fray soon enough."

"Oh, hell! He's going to piss in his pants." Kip grinned at Donaldson's back slightly hunched, swaying off toward the CP van with messages. "Especially when he gets burned for desertion after thinking, all along, that he's been following Flanger's orders."

6

The terraces stepped down toward the Pentagon in wide graceful lines, geometric to a fault as the building they surrounded was. The grass was tight clumped and spongy carpet under his boots. Matthew slipped from the cover of the line of green Army support vehicles, down the turf steps. As the approaching flow of demonstrators blackened the whole of the top north terrace and rumbled toward the cordon lines of troops, Matthew ambled behind the firebreaks of OD green men, his hands jammed into his pockets, unconsciously humming the demonstrators' thunder.

"All we are saying is give peace a chance . . . ."

Cinders and ashes buried Pompeii, not lava flow. And they were here to make ash out of the tribe, right? Right. It was the order of the day: "If them peace nicks fuck up just once--just once, mind you--waste 'em!" After all, they ain't really Americans, anyway. Even their families won't miss the smell. What was his Daddy's last campaign promise? A hippie in every pot . . . boiling? And, he's just been overwhelmingly re-elected Mayor of Roanoke Park, North Carolina, a typical American town.

He had a dream, too. It turned into Tent City. It didn't much matter now that it had been Fort Jackson, South Carolina, not D.C. He believed in God the Father Almighty, maker of heaven and earth, and in Jesus Christ, his only son, our Lord, who was conceived of the Holy Spook, born of the vagina, Mary, suffered under punctilious Pilot, was socialized, died, and buried. On the third day, he was drafted.

"Bat . . . tal . . . I . . . on!" The command echoed down the ranks.

"Com . . . pan . . . y!"

"Pla . . . toon!"

"Squad!"

"Fix ba . . . yo . . . nets!" Shreesh. Long knives scraped against metal as a thousand hands unsheathed a thousand bayonets. Steel clattered as they snapped the bayonets onto noses of M14 and M16 rifles.

"All we are saying is . . . ."

"Bat . . . tal . . . I . . . on!"

"Com . . . pan . . . y!"

"Pla . . . toon!"

"Squad!"

"Pre . . . sent h'arms!"

Ballooning cumulus clouds rolled in from West Virginia. Rifles rattled in cloud-filtered sunlight. Unsteady hands slapped stocks. Metal barrels hitting palms boomed against the clouds.

" . . . . Give peace a chance . . . ."

Two poles. War and peace. Order and chaos. A swirling double helix of human beings. Like Crick and Watson, discover. Like Jefferson and Paine, create. Grow up, for real. March on Washington now that we're a nation of our own. So easy, too. But, the hippies want your soul just as much as A R M Y, I B M, G M C, A B C, C B S, N B C, C O R E, S N C C, N A A C P, K K K, Y A F, S D S, A D A, M I C - K E Y . . . M O U S E.

Pain in Matthew's stomach knocked him to his knees on the spongy turf as if one of these national guardsmen had stuck him with his bayonet. He felt flu-like rushes from his toes, flushing his cheeks, his eyes, his brain. He had believed every fucking word of "Spin and Marty" and look where it got him. His stomach tied up in knots, on his knees in the grass surrounding the fucking Pentagon and in the uniform of his enemy.

To salvage that much from their wreckage on that Cylla and Charybdis shoreline. Just that much only. To ascend from their parents' maelstrom of good intentions with only white hair and a startled look.

"Bat . . . tal . . . I . . . on!"

"Com . . . pan . . . y!"

"Pla . . . toon!"

"Squad!"

"Or . . .der h'arms!"

"Or . . .der h'arms!"

"Or . . .der h'arms!"

"Or . . .der h'arms!"

Again, rifles rattled. This time against their shoulders. Butt plates thudded to the turf. Palms slapped thighs.

We are the basic structural unit on which are founded powerful nations. Out of us came hamlets, mayors, sailors, soldiers, massacres, tribunals, witch trials, pesticides, genocides, the rockets that knocked down Ward's chopper like a hunter shoots down a quail with a twelve-gauge, always using the one thing we know is power to place our own hobby horses in history books.

Fear. A germ in the jungle after all. For the summer's here, and it's time for fighting in the streets, boy. The time is right for valid revolution, if you can find any. Upheavaloution. Thought actualized. Ideas. The ground of all determinations. We are what clusters around the cores of churches, PTA's, Marches of Dimes, prime-time TV, messiahs of all sizes. If we change, if each of us changes, then everything else necessarily changes. When we finally realize that the deliverer isn't coming, it's ourselves we'll have to see slouching toward Manhattan to be born.

Tears began to burn Matthew's cheeks. "Oh, God help us!" He struggled to his knees, then to his feet, stretching his arm toward the marching mob. "It's up to each of us, brothers and sisters. Each of us!"

The flow of demonstrators seemed to dam up a few thousand yards in front of the cordon lines. Matthew approached the troop lines from the rear. His baseball cap tilted low over his eyes creating an impenetrable mask. The Lone Ranger rides again. His eyes had dried. His stomach still hurt. His chest throbbed. "We have to help ourselves," he muttered. His ears rang a steady penetrating

C sharp which he was sure would blow his ear drums out at any moment. "Each of us must change."

He seemed to regain control by the time the guard battalion commander became aware of the temporary stalemate and allowed his soldiers to break ranks. They milled around in clumps of three or four or five, smoking, playing some fast hands of five card stud or gin with soiled, cracked cards. Few traded the expected war stories, for very few, if any, of these guardsmen and reserves had ever been to war.

The demonstrators huddled across the battlefield. Nearly every one of them had been to war, at least on battlefields like Little Rock and Birmingham. The blue X on the Order of Battle map in the van now breathed, perspired, sang. No longer a grease pencil mark on acetate, the X pulled at him like the sun pulls meteorites into it. Thirty-five thousand and growing. He could not help himself any more than those meteorites could help themselves. The X impelled his body through jabbering troops heavy with the smell of fatigues becoming wilted and soggy in the unseasonably hot morning. He skirted bayoneted rifles stacked in teepees. This was insane. He had to do something.

"When in the c . . . course . . . ." His voice cracked as he stepped past the cluster of troops. "When in the course of human events, it becomes necessary for one People to dissolve the Political Bonds which have connected them with another . . . they should declare the causes which impel them in the Separation."

The sun seeped through the cloud cover as Matthew passed beyond the troop lines. Unsnapping the metal catches which held his pistol behind him toward the already jeering mob in OD green. He could hear JAG's charges now: Willful loss of Army property; desertion in the face of the enemy; incitement to mutiny. He turned back to face his comrade-in-arms, cautiously stepping backwards as he continued his recitation. "We hold these Truths to be self-evident, that all M . . . PEOPLE are created equal, that they are endowed by their Creator with certain unalienable Rights, that among these Rights are Life, Liberty, and the Pursuit of Happiness--That to secure these Rights, Governments are instituted among M . . . People, deriving their just Powers from the consent of the Governed, that whenever any Form of Government becomes destructive to these Ends . . . ."

The demonstrators on the terraces began to cheer as his words became understandable to them. "It is the Right of the People to alter or abolish it!" With those words, Matthew fumbled at his left pocket, heavy with the weight of his decorations. He slipped his father's letter out and set it afire with his lighter, waving it above his head. Through the flame and smoke, Matthew could make out a figure in fatigues stumbling madly down the terraces from the line of military support vehicles which almost formed a horizon of their own.

Jesus. Donaldson had mistaken this action for his signal. Guess it was pretty unmistakable at that. At least it couldn't go unnoticed, even by Donaldson.

The great blue X embraced them both with song.

7

"All we are saying is give peace a chance . . . ."

The tribe had been singing ever since Matthew and a handful of demonstrators were arrested at the Pentagon steps. The muffled-by-distance chant was the heart beat of the moment as Colonel Flanger approached Matthew and his guard. The Colonel saluted the MP. "Corporal. As you were."

"Good evening, sir!" He snapped a salute against his helmet that was as crisp as his triple-starched green fatigues without ever letting go of the cuffs behind Matthew's back.

Flanger stepped directly in front of Matthew. His eyes squinted in the half-light and chewed on an unlit cheroot. "Uncuff the prisoner, Corporal!"

"But, sir. Colonel?"

"Don't 'but' me, you . . . ah . . . Corporal." Flanger chomped right through his cheroot.

"But, sir? This is a political prisoner. I have to know your reasons, sir? I'm accountable, sir!"

"I'm a Full Bird Colonel in the United States Army Intelligence Corps. You don't have a clearance high enough, young man. Just obey my order. Now, Corporal!"

Matthew rubbed his wrists involuntarily after the Corporal removed the cuffs. Flanger edged closer to his top sergeant and instructor. He leaned near to his Staff Sergeant's left ear.

"Just tell 'em, Staff Sergeant, that you were following my orders. After all, you were going after that renegade Donaldson, weren't you?"

Colonel Flanger's jaw lines sagged in the shadows of the flashlight beam shooting from the young MP corporal's hand directly into Matthew's haggard, smiling face. He didn't even try to avoid the light. He knew it would be useless anyway. MP's like this corporal would follow his eyes in any direction with the beam. It had something to do with control.

Flanger remembered. At thirteen-thirty hours, Klopps banged on the door of the CP. "Sergeant Parkrow's defected, Colonel, sir!" Of course, he didn't believe even Klopps. Not for a minute! Parkrow had been his most trusted NCO for months now. "You mean Donaldson, don't you, Sergeant Klopps?" That was the plan. But Klopps knew that. It had been his sarcasm that had started the whole damn ball rolling. "No, sir. I mean Matthew, ah, Staff Sergeant Parkrow, sir. But, Donaldson did follow him like a dog after its master, all the time figuring that Matthew's defection to the hippies wasn't really a defection at all. It was his 'unmistakable signal.'"

Flanger poured over Matthew's face in the light. Goddamn it! Of all his troops, why Parkrow? He'd been like a son.

"But, sir?" Matthew shaded his eyes from the blinding light for the first time. He couldn't see the MP behind the flashlight and didn't care. He could barely see an outline of Colonel Flanger's face hanging in the darkness above and beyond the light beam. He couldn't seem to stop his voice from saying what it was about to say. "The plan was for Donaldson to defect at my signal. Not for me to defect. Right?"

Flanger remembered. At seventeen-forty hours, Klopps called his van. "Damn, sir. Matthew's really done it now." Flanger had swallowed hard. "What?"

Static in the patch between vans garbled Klopps' voice for a few seconds. "Repeat, Klopps." He heard Kip clearing his throat.

"They've just arrested over six hundred demonstrators who tried to storm the Pentagon." More static. "And, Matthew Parkrow, Staff Sergeant, U.S. Army Intelligence Command, led the charge!"

"Jesus Christ!"

The silver haired Colonel with a passion for unlit cheroots and brandy shook his head, now, unable to look Matthew in the eyes, even though he knew Matthew could not see him through the glare of the flashlight beam. "You can level with the Corporal, Staff Sergeant Parkrow. You won't be breaking security. I'm giving you permission to say something in your defense here." Flanger tried to catch Matthew's eye and wink at him, but Matthew was staring directly into the light again like a deer mesmerized in the headlights of roadside hunters.

"But, sir. I was already leveling with the Corporal. I led that charge, and I'm proud to admit it!"

"You deserted, you commie bastard!"

"Corporal, that'll be enough. I'll handle this matter with your commander, Major Foldy. Your security clearance isn't high enough for this. You're dismissed!"

"But, Colonel, sir. He's under arrest, sir."

"That's all, young man! Now di di fucking mau, Corporal, before you find yourself suddenly on security patrol along the fucking DMZ!"

In the shadows, the MP snapped his heels together, saluted sharply. "Yes, sir, Colonel, sir!" He flicked the flashlight beam away from Matthew's face and stomped by him. "You'll get yours, fucking commie traitor!" The line of white light bobbed and weaved in front of him as he marched off in the direction of the MP headquarters where fuzzy yellow lights illuminated van windows and seeped through the cracks around the van doors like some kind of smog. "You'll get yours!"

Flanger groped in the darkness left by the departure of the MP Corporal and his flashlight. He touched Matthew's shoulders with his rough but manicured hands. "Staff Sergeant. Ah, Matthew. Listen to me, son. You've only got a matter of days left in this man's Army. An excellent record. Many decorations. Hell, most career soldiers would be envious of all that lettuce you carry above your left pocket. About the only thing missing is the Medal of Honor, and, so I've heard, you should've gotten that instead of that Silver Star." Flanger paused, chewing on his cigar butt that was no longer there.

43

"Son, I can take care of this mess, if you'll just go along with our little story here. Hell, spying on dissidents ain't nothing new. That's why getting rid of Donaldson that way seemed like it would be so easy. Of course, I didn't expect my best NCO to . . . ."

"Oh, well. The Old Man would believe your story, anyway, even if it wasn't backed up by me, his most trusted commander. We infiltrate groups like that all the time. You knew that didn't you?"

"Yes." Matthew shrugged off the Colonel's shaky fingers. "But it's not my story, Colonel. It's yours, and it's a lie."

"You've lied before, Matthew. Everybody has. In fact, you lied to Eddie Donaldson just this morning. Didn't you?"

"Yes. But that was expediency, not a matter of conscience."

"Bull balls, son! Bull balls! This ain't no philosophy 101 class where you can split cunt hairs all day long and never cut your finger. This is real life where cunt hairs are more like piano wires. They just might cut you good, son. JAG'll damned sure cut you no slack at all in these times. They'll hang your young ass, son. Don't you realize that?"

"That's the . . . ." He shuffled his feet, looking at the ground he could only feel beneath his boots but not actually see. "Yes, I do know that, sir."

"Sure!" Flanger snapped his fingers. "Of course, that's it! You want JAG to hang you, don't you, son? That's it! Sure. You want to be drummed out of this man's Army like Chuck Conners in 'Branded.' Right?"

"Me, sir?"

"Yes, son. You!"

"Aw, come on, Otis! I'm not some martyr."

"Then, why?"

"Maybe because they're my people. Not you." He waved toward the yellow cubes of light on the hill that were the windows into the military support vans.   "Or them."

"Oh, you poor young fool."   Flanger reached through the night air and grabbed Matthew's right shirt sleeve. "Don't you understand yet that 'your people' have got to be the people in power, son?"

Gasoline generators hummed and rattled louder, now, filling the silence between them.   "Maybe because they're right."

"Hear that sound, son?"

"What, sir?"

"That rumbling noise?"

"You mean the generators, sir?"

"No, Matthew.   Something different.   The sound of a jeep. It's that MP Corporal's commanding officer's jeep. We've run out of time, you and I. You must decide."

"But, I have already decided, sir."

"Christ, son.   If you persist in this, you'll end up spending the rest of your life looking over your shoulder at every turn. Do you realize that? Do you fully comprehend that, Matthew?"

Matthew could no longer look at Colonel Flanger's face. "I'm sorry, Colonel Flanger. I truly am, sir."

"So am I, Staff Sergeant Parkrow. So am I."

Part Two

The way is an empty vessel

Tao Te Ching

You used to be so amused
at Napoleon in rags
And the language that he used.
Go to him now; he calls you;
you can't refuse.
When you ain't got nothin',
you got nothin' to lose.

How does it feel
to be on your own,
with no direction home
like a rolling stone?

"Like a Rolling Stone," Bob Dylan

8

The day before Bobby was shot in the kitchen of the Hotel Ambassador, the spring semester at Columbia was closing in an uneasy truce that settled over the university like the summer haze of smog and sun that embraced The City. Matthew's court martial convictions for willful loss of government property, desertion in the face of the enemy, and incitement to mutiny, as well as his subsequent dishonorable discharge were six months in his past.

He had completed his first semester in the graduate school on a combination of scholarships and his blood money savings from Viet-Nam. The Court Martial Board couldn't take those things away from him like they had his rights and privileges and benefits. And, all his medals couldn't wipe away his desertion to the hippies.

"No school for you, deserter swine! Not at the expense of this man's Army!

"Guilty! Guilty! Guilty!"

Matthew scuffed his sneakers past the granite sundial along College Walk toward the Amsterdam Avenue gate. Fortunately, Columbia graduate school had taken a different view of his acts of conscience. He muttered thanks to the graduate school admissions board for not only admitting him but for granting him some scholarship and fellowship money and to the invisible Students for a Democratic Society for somehow arranging personal recognizance releases for himself and the more than three hundred brothers and sisters busted at FayerWeather Building.

Two PeterBuilts rumbled side-by-side, snaking through traffic Broadway bound, rattling like worn shock absorbers. Matthew leaned against the gate irons where something like a force field had separated the campus from the streets of Harlem until Martin Luther King was assassinated in Memphis on April 4.

By the fifteenth, there had been riots in Washington, D.C. and over a hundred other cities. By the twenty-third, there was an intellectual riot in Hamilton between the whites and the blacks over who was in charge of the frigging student uprising at Columbia. By the thirtieth, the force field was shattered by charging New York police. "Let the niggers alone; get the freaks in FayerWeather," the police whispered among themselves as they marched past the sundial.

Divide and conquer. Old as Alexander, but the Students African-American Society took the bait of power. It was too easy. It was a "Donaldson."

The pigs were shocked as hell when they kept dragging us out one by one long after they thought that there shouldn't be any more freaks left. Fools, they thought that there was only about three or four hundred students in Hamilton, Low Library, Math, Avery, and FayerWeather all combined. Shit, there were more than that in FayerWeather alone.

After five months in Harlem in a third floor walk-up studio, it still shocked Matthew when he left campus to see so many black faces scrambling along the sidewalks, across 116th Street as the red PeterBuilt cabs with golden streaks along their doors roared by, when there were so few blacks inside those university walls.

As small as their campus numbers were, however, they had certainly taken the initiative in Hamilton. Ran the whites out. The SASers established themselves as the revolutionary leaders of Columbia, a separate militant entity from the SDS. Stunned. Confused. The SDSers weren't going to be expunged from their role in this battle so easily. It had been a long time coming.

"If we can't hang out together, then we'll hang out separately!" And where was there a better place to do that than President Kirk's office in Low Library? He was the one who started the whole fucking chain reaction of power trips, anyway, trying to ram that no inside demonstrations rule down their throats. It was amazing what people will do when they are frustrated or castrated."

"Matthew?"

Honey among smog-constricted throats. "What?" Matthew rubbed the bristles of three days stubble with the back of his right hand as he stopped in the middle of his turn toward 116th Street. "Oh, hey. Is that really you, Emmy Lou?" The lines of her angular face were fuzzy like a photograph washed out by bright sunlight. Her lips and cheeks flushed in the afternoon heat. Her nostrils quivered.

"Yeah, it really is me."

Her jasmine perfume masked out the desperation behind the smells of gasoline and pizza that flooded the avenue and the street.

"I heard that you were in jail, Matthew."

Down the block someone whistled for a cab. Matthew watched a yellow-and-black taxi whip across three lanes of traffic on Amsterdam. Brakes squalled as it slid to a stop in front of Slick Santos, dressed for a circus in his pastel yellow velveteen suit and matching musketeer hat with an ostrich plum stuck in the band, wilting already from the humidity and heat.

The only problem, Slick, is that the circus is over; and you never showed up. Testing a smack buy in Queens, so I've been told. "Yeah, I was. But somebody fixed PR's for everybody."

"Wow. Santos came through?" She motioned at him entering the taxi. "That's far out."

"Not far out at all, Madame Bovary. Only a little out of jail until the trial. Then, who the fuck knows." He shrugged. "I'm afraid I don't have a great deal of faith in our jurisprudence system, military or civilian."

"I heard at the Wherein Doas Cafe that you'd been busted along with everybody else in FayerWeather when the pigs stormed the Sundial People." She crinkled her upturned nose and shaded her blue eyes from the hazy sun behind Matthew's head. "I thought . . . ." She shrugged. "I just got these vibes that I ought to come look for you here, for some reason."

"Yeah. But, it was the SDS that got us out, not fucking Santos. He reneged. When we called the bondsman he'd told us to call, the guy said he never heard of any Santos. And, on top of that, the fucker never even showed up at the station. He denied us three times last night, Madame Bovary. Three times!"

"I guess your father's going to be mad as hell about this, you know?" Emmy Lou tossed her taffy hair off of her shoulders which were damp with sweat down to the sun halter that covered her breasts in blue to match the jeans slung around her slender hips. "He hasn't forgiven you for getting drummed out of the Army yet."

"I know." Averting his eyes from her flat, palpitating stomach, bare and moist in the sun and thoughts of how her body trembled when he touched her navel with his tongue, Matthew fumbled with memories of guilty unless proven innocent, objections, motions for dismissal by his lawyers, rulings and over-rulings. Empty faces with marble eyes. The judges sat at attention. Their gold leaves, silver birds, and golden stars flashed from their collars like sunbursts. Those were his peers? His court martial had been a sunburst, too. Or was that a supernova?

He threw his hands up toward the sun. "His once vote-producing hero son has turned into a vote-losing radical, queer, commie who has been stripped of his rank and honors and marched out the gates of Fort Holabird to the incessant snare of drums like Chuck Conners in 'Branded.' Jason believes I'm a complete failure." He leaped into the air and landed in a sloppy pirouette on the sidewalk, shrieking. "And, look at me, Madame Bovary! I'm proving him to be exactly right, aren't I?" As he began to stumble, Emmy Lou hugged him to her, her perspiration dampening the T-shirt she had tie-dyed purple for him as their stomachs pressed together. Matthew steadied himself against her, pulling her tight thighs against his. "Why don't we do it in the road?"

"I think my place's better than the middle of Amsterdam Avenue, Matthew." Emmy Lou stuck the tip of her tongue between his lips. She loved to lure his tongue into her mouth, then, nip it. "At least, it's air-conditioned."

9

Darkness at the break of noon
Shadows even the silver spoon
The handmade blade, the child's balloon
Eclipses both the sun and moon
To understand you know too soon
There is no sense in trying.

Sandalwood incense smoldered in the hollow of a tiny bronze mushroom. "There's no need for you to go to the Cafe if that's all you're going for, Matthew." Emmy Lou's hair fell like shredded shadows over Bottechelli breasts as she adjusted the position of the mushroom--a little to the left of the Garrard changer. Dylan's nasal sounds bounced from the modular steel shelves she'd purchased at the Sears mail order outlet in downtown Manhattan. Imagine? She'd only had to look up the phone number in the Manhattan Yellow Pages Directory, dial it, and place her order.

"You can pick it up here or send a check and we'll deliver via the mail," the Dietrich voice of the clerk had informed her.

"Please, send the order by mail. I'll get the check out today." Funds were no problem. Jason was very generous to her. She wasn't at all sure why. After all, she was merely the maid's niece. And, he didn't help Matthew at all, and he was his blood son. Matthew, however, helped himself.

Pointed threats, they bluff with scorn
Suicide remarks are torn
From the fool's gold mouthpiece
The hollow horn plays wasted words
Proves to warn
That he not busy being born
Is busy dying.

She'd lined her studio apartment's off white walls with Beatles White Album photos, posters of Buddy Holly, Bob Dylan in black leather, Jimi Hendrix setting his guitar on fire at Monterey Pop, Janice Joplin, Che Guevera rattling a rifle in his left hand, Jerry Rubin smoking a joint in his right hand in front of the gymnasium at his old Cincinnati high school, Eldridge Cleaver leaving jail or going to jail, and a hand-painted sign--SDS--in day-glo red on dull black cardboard which she'd added to her wall collection as soon as she'd heard about Matthew's bust.

Until then, she still hadn't been sure how far Matthew would go for politics, ideologies, truth, beauty, revolution. The fact was, there were a lot of people around who hadn't been sure either, even after what he'd done at the Pentagon rally. You could never be too careful when it came to who might be an undercover government agent rather than what they seemed to be, even when you've known them all of your life. Hell, especially if you've known them all your life. Before, she knew Matthew like you come to know a tree you climb every day or a prayer you say each night. You know the bark or the words but not the sap or the meaning. This semester she had come to know something of Matthew's true sap, something of what his words really meant. Now, she was sure. She trusted him. She respected him.

I . . . love him.

"What do you mean, Emmy Lou?"

"About what?"

"About not needing to go to the Cafe ?" His fingers floated over Emmy Lou's thighs, her firm buttocks.

"Fiend." She reached behind and slapped at Matthew's hand. "Stay on that mattress! Don't waste all that testosterone on a woman when she's walking away from you." She giggled as she skipped out of his reach, following wisps of incense smoke toward the kitchenette at the far end of the apartment where the refrigerator whirred and the air-conditioning wheezed in the ninety-four-degree heat. It was already proving to be a long, hot summer even with air-conditioners.

In the black light violet of the room, her muscles rolled like a DiVinci drawing, creating velvet shadows on her golden skin. Her hair, now flung over her shoulders, splashed down her back to her hips like copper strands.

"Want a Bud?"

"Sure."

She opened the door. The white light glared like a sun a million light years away in nova or an MP's flashlight in the darkness. Her body seemed to melt for an instant. She fumbled for two cans of beer. Her sculptured lean curves disappeared as she slammed the door and snuffed out the light.

"So, what *do* you mean?" Waiting for her answer, he reached above him for the stone hash pipe on the night table behind the head end of the mattress lying on the floor. His fingers also located a small piece of tin foil containing the last of their Lebanese blonde.

One tab swishpopped on the kitchen counter, then the other. Emmy Lou tossed the aluminum tabs into a Dietsch grocery bag leaning against the wall next to her fridge. She turned with the beers in her hands and slinked back across the shag carpet toward the mattress, singing along with Dylan.

Temptation's page flies out the door
You follow, find yourself at war
Watch waterfalls of pity roar
You feel to moan but unlike before
You discover that you'd just be
One more person crying.

"Quick! Something's burning!" Matthew choked out the words as he held in smoke and offered Emmy Lou the warm stone pipe. It glowed amber in the muffled violet light.

So don't fear if you hear
A foreign sound to your ear
It's alright, Ma, I'm only sighing.

She traded him one Bud for the pipe, took a long hit, and flopped beside him on the sheets. Matthew clamped the can of beer between his bare knees. He shivered momentarily from the coldness of the aluminum, then finished the pipe and tapped the pipe bowl on the Holiday Inn ash tray on the night table. He refilled it with another pinch of hash. "Here, Madame Bovary. Have another hit." He pushed the cardboard drawer from its matching blue box cover, selected a safety match, shoved the Ohio Blue Tip cover back over the drawer containing the few remaining kitchen matches, replaced the box on the night table. Then, he snapped the pale blue tip on his left thumbnail. The match flared in the dim light.

"Where did you learn that one, boy?" She sucked on the cooling stone as he held the match over the top of the bowl. Hot sweet smoke tickled her lungs. She coughed as she tried to hold the smoke in and handed the still-smoking pipe back to Matthew. He finished it as she sucked on her beer, a luxurious sigh swelling in her chest.

"Not down home, honey, that's for sure. They only know how to strike matches on their tar heels."

"My, my." She smacked her lips and tickled his feet. He jumped. "Now, ya'll know that ain't so, boy."

Blood rushed from his shocked feet, following her hot fingers up his calves, behind his knees, along his inner thighs. Her hands cradled his testicles as she bent over him. Her amber breasts stretched toward him as if to embrace him. "Christ, this dope's clearly for fucking under the influence of . You know?"

"I know," she purred. She arched her back as he feather-touched the undersides of her breasts with electric fingers, stroking up to her nipples, but not yet touching them. Her breath snagged in her throat with every completed caress.

His tongue touched the tip of her left nipple. It was so engorged that it might have been hard enough to play albums. She slippery slid over him.

"Oh, Matthew!"

Their lips touched, parted. Their tongues rolled around one another. A part of Matthew seemed to perch on the night table, leaning against the ash tray. Jesus, all that slobbering, swallowing each other's spit. Uggh! Licking sweaty skin coated with The City's smog. A deadly affair, fucking. Shit, you never see Romeo and Juliet or Rogers and Astair or Roy and Dale and Trigger or Tonto and Kimosabi fucking, bucking, sucking. Not only did they not go to the bedroom, but they also did not go the bathroom, unless they had to get their raincoats to face another night of frigid drizzle on the range. No, that would be the mud closet or the medicine cabinet, places where the raincoats of various kinds are stored.

Matthew shuddered. Emmy Lou trembled. Matthew convulsed. Emmy Lou convulsed. They felt like they were collapsing in snow. Becoming one with it. Clinging together, they rolled onto their sides, trembling, then quiet, then trembling again, somewhat less each time.

10

You lose yourself, you reappear.
You suddenly find you got nothing to fear.
Alone you stand with nobody near
When a trembling distant voice, unclear
Startles your sleeping ears to hear
That somebody thinks they've really found you.

"Whew!" He eased out of her and reached for his Winstons on the parson's table. This time he used the striking surface on the side of the Ohio Blue Tip box. The match flared blueorange. He lit his cigarette, then smothered the flame with the smoke he spat out between his lips. He dropped the charred matchstick over his head into the ash ray. "So, is this why," he yawned, stretching from his toes, "I don't need to go out tonight?"

Emmy Lou returned his smile, then pinched his right inner thigh just below his groin.

"Ouch!"

"That's only one part of it, Mr. Parkrow!" She curled her buttocks against his stomach, her head in the crook of his right arm. Beyond her flowing hair, her jasmine scent, hanging on the wall was her latest art class project--a painting of sixteen virgins dressed in habits of seaweed. Their ghostly heads seemed more like skulls peering from beneath heavy hoods than real faces as they bowed in prayer around an upper room like table similar to the one the disciples gathered around in "The Last Supper." Their shrouds were streaks of black and green overlapping, mixing. The table cloth gleamed as white as their skulls. "The other part is that I have another lead on that guy you hope might be Ward."

A question in your nerves is lit
Yet you know there is no answer fit
To satisfy, insure you not to quit

to keep it in your mind and not forgit
That it is not her or she or them or it
That you belong to.

"What?"

"Yeah. Some guys down at Wherein Doas finally believed your story. I guess because you got busted yesterday. Until then, just about everybody at the Cafe was still suspicious that you might be undercover FBI, CIA, or some kind of special operations intelligence somebody trying to find this guy and bust him.

Although the masters make the rules
For the wise men and the fools
I got nothing, Ma, to live up to.

"Everyone there's been paranoid ever since old man Henderson Crampton came snooping around last year. I wish I'd never told him, you know, that I'd seen this guy who looked like Ward. But, I really felt so sorry for the old guy what with his wife dead and all. Weakness of mine, I must admit. He was up here for some doctors convention or something. Called me up. Took me to dinner. I just couldn't bear watching him break down in front of me, dribbling huge tears onto the dark bread in the Brocheteria at Eighty-sixth. Then all of a sudden you show up. It spooked them.

"Anyway, Marty, the owner, he said that this guy was real secretive about who he was and all, and he split as soon as Ward's father came nosing around."

"Shit, that's a really cold trail by now.

"Not as cold as you might think. Come to find out, the reason he was so spooked was because he's supposedly some big shit underground leader, and the heat's after him all the time. They're continually trying to set him up for some kind of bust or another. And, the reason the trail's not cold, honey, is that Marty's pretty sure that this guy will be at the demonstration in Chicago."

"That's coming up soon. Maybe I should . . . ."

"Do you have to go after him, Matthew? Why couldn't you just finally let this thing go and spend the rest of the summer between these thighs?" She rolled over to face him and pushed her mound against him. Her eyes were agates in the black-lighted room, a pouting smile nibbling at the edges of her lips. "We both know that Ward Crampton died in a helicopter crash in Viet-Nam."

"No *we* don't!" He fumbled behind for another Winston and lit it quickly. The smoke curled blue spirals and helixes toward the ceiling. "What *we* do know is fuck, argue; argue, fuck. Fuck; argue; fuck."

"Well, doesn't that beat the hell out of most things?"

"Like what?"

"Like playing doctor down in the hole at twilight when everything was lavender. The pines swished in the evening breezes."

"Is the hole covered over yet?"

"No, it's still there. In fact, when I was down to visit Aunt Alecia last month, I spent an entire afternoon sitting down near the sewer pipe we used to pretend was a cavern. Remember?"

"Yeah."

"I just sat there soaking up memories and the good old North Carolina spring sun. There isn't anything like that here."

"I know. Probably the closest is the Cloisters."

Emmy Lou wriggled on top of Matthew, basking in the warmth of his body like she had in the warmth of that sun and those memories of when they were children and their world was still full of rabbits and sparrows and black snakes and miles of pine forests they had roamed for what, then, seemed would be forever.

"Little by little he's killing it all, you know?"

"I know that, too."

"But no one can take away what we once had, Madame Bovary--you and me and Ward and old Turkey Locklear."

"I get this awful feeling sometimes, Matthew--you know, right here in the pit of my tummy like a kind of morning sickness only it strikes at any time of the day or night--that we're all that's left of the old Roanoke Park, the only organisms that haven't yet been gobbled up by civilization as we know it." Her words trailed into the whirring silence of the air-conditioned apartment three flights up at 201 East 83rd Street.

Matthew felt the wet warmth of her tears on his chest. He stroked taffy waves that fell down her back and leaned up to kiss her salty cheeks. "We may be, Madame Bovary. We, very well, may be." His eyes glazed over like a high jumper readying for his approach to the bar. The slightest touch and the bar might fall. He blanked his mind except for the quivering, intense creature now devouring his being. He'd known her, it seemed, forever. Ever since Alecia had brought her to live with them after a three-month vacation with her relatives down east near Williamston. He vaguely remembered the pink bunting she was wrapped in that day. In those times, he was only aware of a baby in the house. Alecia's niece.

"At least we've got each other, now. That musn't ever change, Matthew."

"For sure, Emmy Lou. For sure." He snubbed out the half-smoked Winston and snuggled under her weight down into the bed.

Walk upside-down inside handcuffs
Kick my legs to crash it off
Say okay, I have had enough
What else can you show me?

And if my thought-dreams could be seen
They'd probably put my head in a guillotine
But it's alright, Ma, it's life, and life only.

"Let's get a little shut-eye, what you say?"

"Okay. If you really think you can sleep with this hot body beside you." She slipped from the mattress to the hardwood floor, bounced to the record changer and flicked the switch to off. Then, she snapped off the black light and crawled back between the sheets, snuggling close to Matthew's back.

"The only name he ever used was Crayon."

"Who?"

"The dude that looks like Ward."

"Crayon? Must be a nickname." Matthew scratched his lightly bearded chin. "Guess I'll have to go to Chicago and find out what color Crayola this guy really is, huh?"

Emmy Lou sighed. She pulled him closer to her. "Not tonight, I hope." She kissed him and fell asleep almost immediately.

Three hours later he couldn't find any paper in the dark. He hadn't been able to sleep, thinking about Crayon in Chicago and him, maybe, being Ward. Could it be possible after all this time? He might not even know it, himself. Matthew knew that he had to find out. He prayed that she would understand. No, he knew that she would. Matthew tip-toed out of her apartment, leaving a hasty note scribbled on the back of the Dylan album jacket.

Dearest Madame Bovary,
Sorry to fuck and argue and run. Going after Crayon.
See you in a few weeks.
Matthew

11

Exerpts from
Matthew Parkrow's Notebooks--1968

Then the sands will roll out
A carpet of gold
For your weary toes to be a-touchin',
And the ship's wise men
Will remind you once again
That the whole wide world is watchin'.

January 23. The U.S.S. Pueblo and its eighty-three-man crew were seized by the North Koreans in the Sea of Japan. The crew is accused of electronic spying.
The whole world's watching! The whole world's watching! The whole world's watching!

February 28. Viet-Cong and North Vietnamese regulars hit thirty south Vietnamese provincial capitols in a Tet Offensive. They occupied the U.S. Embassy in Sai-Gon for more than six hours before airborne troops landed on the roof and worked their way to the ground floor, clearing the building of enemy sappers. Tan Son Nhut Air Base was closed by enemy fire to all but combat air traffic. As a result of this Chinese New Year offensive, record military casualties were sustained and more than three hundred and fifty thousand were left homeless refugees, many of whom wandered into the alleys of Sai-Gon and Cho-Lon with only the rags on their backs. The street fighting ended in Hue on February 24.

March 31. In this critical election year, President Lyndon Johnson declined to run for another term as his party's nominee, leaving the field open to Senators Eugene McCarthy and Robert Kennedy .... The people marching in the streets have brought down an arrogant President.

Back to standing in line like everybody else, Baines!
Thomas Jefferson waits for you!

The whole world's watching! The whole world's watching! The whole world's watching!

12

" . . . . But you will all know what I am full of, if you don't see me on other marches," The Reporter concluded. He was the last of the artists and writers to speak. All around Matthew people cheered his words which careened out of the microphone on the band shell stage. A young speaker in a fringed leather vest took the podium after The Reporter had finished his speech.

Matthew closed his pocket-sized spiral notebook and stuffed it into the right pocket of his jeans, patting it in place, then checking the left pocket for his wallet. At night, during his court martial proceedings, when everyone else slept, he would slip into the latrine where the lights were always burning and smoke a joint or two on the shitter while transferring every word from his military notebook into the new spiral one he had purchased at the Fort Holabird PX. He was afraid that the Army would try to confiscate his military notebook. They didn't disappoint him. By the time he had to give the notebook up, however, he had completed the transfer. His wallet was still in place. He thought he might've lost it in all the commotion.

"We ought to know already what you're full of, Mr. Reporter," he sneered as The Reporter, squeezing his way through the webs of hippies surrounded by Black Panthers, stumbled against Matthew's shoulder. "The fight's now, old man, not at the next march!" Matthew startled himself that he spoke directly at The Reporter. After all, here was a writer revered by himself and his fellow students over the years. "Just look at all their hardware, man! Just look around you, Mr. Reporter!" He leaped at The Reporter's white collar. "This is Armies of the Night, Part Two." His head reeled from morning hash as several panthers tore his fingers from The Reporter's shirt and throat, shoving him to the ground. "You know, man, like Toppsie!"

"Hey, man, be cool. Be cool," his black brothers urged as they held him down. "Make love, not war, brother," one of the Yippie guards soothed. The Reporter straightened his collar and brushed off his shirt, gazing distractedly through the crowd toward flashing neon lights of a bar beyond the barbed wire barricades across the street.

Matthew wanted to . . . . "My God, man! We are at war!" He wanted to smash that Yippie's cat-licked face in, to tear out the Panthers' fangs, to rip off the old Reporter's balls, that is if he could find them. He glared into the sweat-stained face of another Yippie guard holding his right arm down. "They all got to go, stupid! Not just the politicians, but the tit-fingered writers too!"

Three hippie nymphs who looked like they'd been cloned from the Blind Faith album cover smothered him in the grass with choruses of strokes and kisses.

"Be mellow, man. Be mellow," they chorused.

"Make love, man, not war, man ."

"Be mellow. Make love."

Matthew writhed against them as they replaced the force of his brothers with their own straight jacket of softness and flesh. His struggles against their restraint made them believe that he was getting worked up sexually. So, Nina, the youngest at seventeen, talked him into walking with her to the river, hoping to divert his attentions. Cool him out. Save him from himself.

The young speaker who replaced The Reporter at the podium had tears in his eyes. He pleaded for silence over the din of the masses. "Please, brothers and sisters, I have something important to say to you. Please."

Matthew hesitated, his eyes locked to the speaker's eyes as he struggled to sit up. He stood up by holding to Nina's tanned shoulders.

"Our brothers and sisters in Czechoslovakia have been completely mauled by the Russians. In France, our brothers and sisters have been placated by shrewd old DeGaulle reforms. The Mexican government is planning to gun down our brothers and sisters in the streets of Mexico City if there's any trouble during the upcoming Olympics. The revolution is left on our shoulders now! We stand alone! It is up to each of us." He shoved his right fist above his head, his long black hair flowing down his neck past his shoulders like a shadow. "Power to the people!"

"Power to the people!" shouted the front rows of the just-hushed crowd.

"Power to the people!" The young speaker thrust his fist again into the demi-shadows of the band shell.

"Power to the people!" the masses echoed.

Matthew felt the power surge through his body like acid. "Power to the people," he yelled along with the hippie girl, Nina, whom he clung to and with all the other sweaty, sticky people surrounding him in the park.

"Power to your prick," Nina giggled softly into Matthew's ear. She squeezed his crotch. The throng erupted. Matthew allowed Nina to drag him from the park, through the streets choked with demonstrators and citizens of Chicago where the power of the Daley machine lined the curbs: troop trucks, Daley's Dozers, barbed wire barricades attached to jeeps to mow them down like trees on a construction site, knots of National Guardsmen surrounding the Hilton.

"What do you expect from him?" Nina's voice cooed like a turtledove amidst the revving of truck engines and the clamor of steel butts of rifles against the concrete streets and sidewalks.

"Expect out of whom?"

"The Reporter."

"Him?" Matthew spit at a truck tire jammed against the curbing. "Exactly what I got . . . . Nothing!" They walked faster to get past the clumps of soldiers. "I used to be one of them," he muttered, nodding his head towards six soldiers bent over a poker game at the corner of the Hilton. "But, I quit."

"A National Guardsman?" She looped his arm in her's and squeezed it against the heat of her contained under a blue work shirt she wore loose, with the shirt tail out flopping over her jean-covered hips.

"No." He forced a smile. She was, after all, trying to be very nice to him. And, she had saved him from probably getting his skull cracked or something equally undesirable. That Yippie and those two Panther dudes would've at least tried if he'd been able to get back up and tear at The Reporter's jugular vein with his teeth like he wanted so desperately to do. "I was the real thing as Henry James would've said."

As her violet eyes that gleamed like polished stones clouded over, small wrinkles etched their sockets. Her rainbow lips drooped and quivered ever so slightly. "Viet-Nam and all that?" Her contralto voice broke.

"That's why I'm here. At least that's part of it."

"You've got more right than anybody. Ah, what is your name, anyway?"

"Matthew."

"A biblical name, huh?"

"Yeah, my father's a religious nut among other fanaticisms."

She laughed with him. "I'm Nina."

"Yeah, I know. I heard one of the other chicks call you that when you all had been pinned down in the park."

"Sorry about that, Matthew, but we were afraid you'd get hurt."

"It's okay, Nina. I probably would've." He paused and lit a Winston. "Or worse, I would've hurt somebody."

"You know, Matthew, if you'd rather, we can go to this pad down the block here. Some fiends . . . ." Her laughter interrupted herself. "I mean, some *friends* of mine have a place there, and I've got a key."

"Sure. Beats the hell out of this heat. Long as we're back at Grant Park in time for the march."

"Sure, baby," Nina crooned against his shoulder as she nestled her shagged auburn hair against him.

They walked along the river bank toward her friends' apartment. Her hair smelled of Dr. Bronner's pure Castille peppermint soap and of hash hish.

"Sure. Just don't be so uptight, baby. We'll do some dope, take a hot bath, and maybe get it on a little."

He could feel her face smiling against his shoulder as they strolled along. "I'm hip to that, Nina. I'm sure as hell hip to that." He knew he'd have to struggle against the straps of Nina's sensuality, maybe even snap them, to get back to Grant Park on time. But, he had to be there. Some McCarthy people had told him earlier that they'd seen a guy setting up one of the aid stations--they couldn't remember exactly where--who looked just like the picture of Ward he had shown them. After all this time . . . and nothing. He wasn't about to miss out on a lead like that. He'd be at Grant Park tonight, for sure. Matthew clung to this thought like he, later, clung to Nina's herb scented thighs.

13

Exerpts from
Matthew Parkrow's Notebooks--1968

April 14. The Reverend Doctor Martin Luther King, Jr. was allegedly assassinated by James Earl Ray (an escaped convict) in Memphis, Tennessee on April 4. President Lame Duck Johnson called in National Guardsmen and federal troops to quell the riots in Washington, D.C., Raleigh, N.C. and one hundred and twenty-five other cities . . . .

The whole world's watching! The whole world's watching! The whole world's watching!

May 10. Preliminary peace talks on Viet-Nam began after a thirty-four-day impasse on the selection of the site for the talks and the shape of the table . . . the goddamned shape of the negotiating table! During this impasse, hundreds of soldiers were killed and wounded and thousands of civilians were rendered homeless and helpless.

July 4. The nuclear submarine Scorpion and its full complement of 99 crew have been presumed lost, like the Thresher, like Ward.

Senator Robert F. Kennedy, well on his way to the Democratic nomination for President after victories in South Dakota and California and the only remaining hope and rallying point for black, white, Indian, Asian, Hispanic, poor, disenfranchised, was murdered by Sirhan Beshara Sirhan in the Hotel Ambassador in Los Angeles. Roosevelt Greer caught the squirrelly bastard; he never made a better tackle.

Kill the man and you kill the idea. Such absurdity!

Remember how in the old westerns, when they had a supposed "killer" stallion on their hands that really wasn't a "killer" stallion but the bad guys wanted everyone to think that he was one, they would inevitably corner the stallion and put him in a situation where he would have to kill or maim in self-defense. Then they would claim that this proved he was truly a "killer" stallion. Well, that plot seems to play out okay with people, too. Anybody, no matter how passive they want to be and try to be can only be pushed so far.

The damn has burst!

14

"The whole world's watching! The whole world's watching! The whole world's watching!" the mass chanted as it swirled and swelled against dams of troops surrounding Grant Park. Their candles flickered like a mammoth necklace of molten jewels clinging to a black throat. Nina guided Matthew through the swaying, sweating throng which seemed almost as one organism. His notebook was safely snug in his jeans, and Nina's friend's Nikon hung around his neck and over his shoulder, swinging back and forth across his left hip. *So you think you want a revolution, we-ell....*

"Just pretend you want an interview with him, Matthew. That way you'll get a chance to talk to him up close and personal." Nina's violet eyes sparkled like capsules suspended in her upside down pill bottle face. He'd made the analogy first when Nina turned that aspirin bottle containing two black beauties over, popping them into her hand that popped them into her mouth. That instant when the hits of speed began to drop from the bottom of the overturning bottle was when the powdery glass reminded him of the shape of her face and the pills, of her eyes.

Man, what luck. Damn. She was this Crayon dude's old lady, sort of. She thought the pictures he showed her were of Crayon. Didn't believe that he was Ward, though. She said he was from Billings, Montana. That he went to Berkeley. Got his start in underground politics in the Free Speech Movement. Never went to Viet-Nam as far as she knew. He was opposed to the war. But, what the fuck did Nina know? She'd only been with him for a few months. He knew that he must talk to this Crayon directly.

"I'll make like an interviewer for the *Rolling Stone.* No?"

"Yeah. That's hip. But, Crayon really digs *The Voice.*"

"That's cool. *The Village Voice.* That's it! I'll be a reporter for *The Voice.*"

"Hey, look who's coming, Matthew." Nina's slender fingers waved toward a large table on the grass at the edge of the park. The Reporter reeled forward and struggled with a bull horn. Nina suddenly wrapped her arms around Matthew, squeezing her body close, her lips brushing his right ear. "You're not still gonna tear out his jugular vein, are you?"

"No."

"That's good, baby, 'cause Crayon ought to be showing up here any minute now, and he just loves The Reporter."

"Crayon loves The Reporter?"

"Yeah, man. He really does. He's read everything that man's ever written."

"We all have, and we all used to love him, Nina."

Matthew and Nina pushed through the last three row-like clusters of people surrounding the table. The Reporter paused, glanced his way. Was there some recognition hidden behind those blood-shot, cataracting eyes? The Reporter was cleverly setting it up so that he wouldn't have to march with them tonight against Daley's thugs. If he could only get three hundred of the conventioneers in the Democratic Convention to march with him, he said. Then, he promised, he would march with them. Oh, yes, then he'd march through the Daley Dozers and the Daley thugs and the National Guard even through Dante's Inferno. Oh, yes!

Of course, that would be impossible. People were already scared shitless of repercussions from THEM and revolution from US. He'd never pull together three conventioneers much less three hundred, and he knew it! Poor convention fuckers, dilemma-riddled, waiting for Godot.

Matthew stopped to watch The Reporter return the bull horn to the table and stumble off through the crowd. Matthew's head slumped for a moment. "Jesus, I really feel sorry for him."

"Who?"

He nodded toward the table and toward where walls of people had already closed around the path The Reporter had shoved through them like a fast-healing wound. "The Reporter."

"But, I thought you wanted to kill him?"

"Not any more. I just don't want to have to look at him."

Suddenly, Nina squealed. "Crayon!" She dodged a knot of hippies on the right side of the table and leaped into what seemed to be Ward Crampton's arms. "Crayon, baby! What's happening, man?" The tall, lanky man smothered her words with long kisses.

Ward or Crayon, he was obviously happy to see little Nina. Then, who wouldn't be? Hell, she gave everything, took only a little speed. Didn't even have to feed her.

Matthew pushed his way through the growing clump of hippies by the table as a dozen Panther security guards slipped closer to the platform. So far, so good, he thought. No replay of Columbia. Not yet, anyway. If we could only realize why *"Peter Pan"* hasn't played in fifteen years on TV or at the movie houses, then we'd understand why we can be strong, can survive, maybe even prevail as Faulkner said between benders.

The young man Nina called Crayon was rangy in his patched Wranglers and rainbow work shirt. His face was one of those square-jawed, blue-chinned types Matthew would have expected to see sauntering along Madison or Park Avenues or along Wall Street in subdued pinstripes. Except for his auburn hair being pulled behind his neck in a long ponytail, he looked exactly like Ward's photographs which Matthew always carried in his wallet. This was just plain eerie, he thought. He felt like he was about to interview the man he had driven to his death over six years before. As he emerged from the knot of people, Nina spotted him. She waved and began dragging the young man toward him.

Matthew's eyes focused on Nina and Crayon scuffling in his direction. The people seemed to congeal around the edges of the open space just past the Panthers and the hippies massed to the right of the improvised stage, ringing the three of them with the white iridescence of their candles. He sensed their closeness to each other in the way their hands clasped, fingers entwined, only loosening as they neared where he stood, transfixed in the white circle of light.

Instinctively, but without ever having had such instincts before, Matthew unsnapped the leatherette camera case dangling against his hip. The front fell open, exposing the camera's covered lens. He popped off the lens cover, adjusted focus, ASA, shutter speed. Then, he dropped to his right knee and began clicking shots of them until they stopped only a few steps away. He smiled at them through the single reflex lens. "What's happening?"

"Crayon, this is Matthew. He's a reporter for the *Village Voice*. He wants to do an interview with you or something." Nina began shoving him toward Matthew's outstretched hand.

Crayon balked. "Yeah? You for real, man?"

"Oh, come on, Crayon, baby. Come on now. Don't be like that. He's a nice enough guy with a job to do."

Crayon's perse eyes seemed like holes in his head in the circle of dull, creamy light. Matthew shivered in the muggy Chicago night although it was far from cool.

There's no way to know where it starts, a shiver. >Sensation >Reaction >Thought >Action >Results. You can pick it up anywhere, it seems. Just like an itch. You sense the itch; your hand scratches; you think: I've got an itch. You put calamine lotion on the irritated skin; the itching stops. Consequently, you feel no more itching; therefore you no longer scratch your skin. You think: I no longer have an itch. You begin pecking at the keys of your antique Underwood elite (all your mother left you); you describe the process you've just experienced.

"Come on, Crayon. Be cool, baby."

Nina reminded him of Emmy Lou's passion and softness. Awash in space. Sharp breath. Helpless, helpless, helpless.

Sucked up between her briny lips. Life ring on this angered sea.

Crayon finally clasped the back of Matthew's hand. Their thumbs hooked. His wiry lips rippled in a hesitant smile. "Matthew?"

"Crayon."

"Yeah, man. Folks started calling me that after Nina tie-dyed this shirt for me."

Matthew fumbled with the camera in his left hand. "What's happening?"

"Not much, man. Just getting it on with this little revolution of ours, man, you know?" Crayon's slender, callused fingers searched his left shirt pocket for cigarettes. He extracted a Lucky Strike and lit it off of Nina's lighter which she had waiting for him. "Thanks, baby." He turned back to Matthew, still scrutinizing him. "You know, man, I don't much like that picture-taking shit. I mean, there're warrants out on me in twelve fucking states!" He paused, dragging deeply on his Lucky. "You dig?"

"Sure, man. I dig. I'm sorry, man. Just trying to get some candid shots, you know." He grasped the camera again which he had let drop back onto his hip. "Here, man, I can pull the film out right now," he continued. He popped the back of the Nikon open and reached for the film inside with his fingers.

"Hey, no, man. Like, that's cool. If it's really for *The Voice*, that's cool."

Matthew closed the camera, letting it drop again to his hip. The people surrounding them surged forward like a wave that has crested and rushes toward the shore. The ring of light shattered into a thousand small flickers.

"You'll have to interview him later, Matthew," Nina interrupted. "The march is starting." She winked at Matthew and clung to Crayon's left arm and Matthew's right.

"He's not the guy I'm looking for, Nina," Matthew whispered, "but thanks. I owe you both. I'll clear things up with Crayon after the march. Okay?"

"That's cool, Matthew. That's real cool."

The mass of demonstrators carried them toward the barricades around the park, manned by the National Guardsmen. Their terrified young faces glowered in the candle light like devil masks formed from fire and deep dark shadows. As the mass swayed and stumbled forward in the tide of the march beginning, they were surrounded by low hoarse voices:

"The whole world's watching."

Matthew wasn't sure if he'd made himself clear to Nina. The chanting had become instant thunder, erupting from Grant park. He took up the chant with the others.

"The whole world's watching. The whole world's watching! The whole world's watching!"

Invisible people shoved lighted candles into their hands. Matthew held his candle aloft with his left hand. His right hand clenched in a fist, he thrust above his head.

"The whole world's watching!"

The march on the Amphitheater was going down.

15

Exerpts from
Matthew Parkrow's Notebooks--1968

August 15. Greensboro, Salem, Montgomery, Watts led to Washington and our storming the Pentagon for peace. That was the newest rallying cry for a people having so few of them left. Race and war sometimes equal genocide . . . always equal genocide. That's what war is: the anthropomorphization of the previous generation's fears of their own progeny, the same cunning which motivates the male guppy to gorge on its own offspring. By sixty-seven, the fears had become blatant!

On February 29, 1968, the Kerner Commission Report cited white racism as the primary cause for black violence which is ripping apart U.S. cities. No reports cited anything as the cause for young, white rebellion now rampant on our campuses. They're killing us off in Memphis, in Los Angeles, but we paralyzed Columbia, didn't we, Goddamn it! Power to the people!

Students struck the spark at the University of Nanterre which led to ten million workers striking in France, paralyzing the country. Like Ghandi did it in South Africa and in India.

If only we could wield such power . . . such united power . . . .

"The whole world's watching!"

As we sit here in a Chicago precinct cell, we know we stand alone, just like the dude on the speaker's stand in Grant Park had said earlier. The sentence of death hangs over every head in Amerika not sporting the proper hair cut.

Death is a way of life here; justice has been its first victim-- long-haired justice, holding scales in its hands to blindly weigh out the marijuana to determine misdemeanor or felony. Established political leaders have been brutally gunned down in our streets. We have been split by superficial differences into black and white camps, thanks to the training of the beasts, the power piggies!

Not until Columbia did they see the advantage in coming down hard on the whites and playing it sort of easy on the blacks. After all, we should've known better. When you revolt, at least do so with clean buildings. Keep them clean while you're occupying them, right? And, of course, the blacks were clean as Amos and Andy during the Columbia riots. Hell, they had the heritage, the knowledge, of being massa's janitors, not us. We were cleaned up after. We weren't expected to clean, ourselves. Then, we get into a frigging revolution, and the powers expect us, all of a sudden, to start cleaning up after ourselves. Jesus!

Hell, the blacks wanted the real leadership, anyway. They wanted it really bad. So, why not give it to them? the beasts reasoned. They would show the revolutionary little white bastards where it was really, truly at . . . . Right?

What the alumni and administration didn't count on was that we'd close down Columbia anyway . . . in spite of our differences. What does that mean? Where does that all lead? Somewhere passed tonight's battle, that's for sure. Nobody takes the least bit of piggy's power and gets away with it. The university, the parent, is dead. Long live the university, the parent!

The whole world's watching!

16

"So, Crayon. I'm really sorry about my little deception, man. But, I'm really desperate to find my friend, if he's still alive." Matthew grasped the cell bars in frustration. He had real problems with being confined.

"It was really all my fault, baby." Nina leaned against the carbondium-like bars which, at least temporarily, defined their universe. "I believed his story about this friend that was missing in action in Viet-Nam and all and that he really believed you might be that friend. Hell, Crayon, he showed me a picture that I would've sworn was you. And you've always been so secretive about your past. Anyway, I remembered him from the March on Washington and his court martial and all. So, man, I believed him. But I just knew that you would be too paranoid to believe such a story. So." She shrugged against the bars. "We came up with this idea of Matthew posing as a *Village Voice* reporter. It was harmless, man."

"Hey, it's okay, baby. Look around you. We're all in this place together. We know each other in the only way that counts."

"Right on, Crayon," Matthew muttered, extending his hand.

"Right fucking on, Matthew!" He grasped the offered hand, locking thumbs and wrapping their fingers around each other's hand in the handshake of the revolution. "You know, man, speaking of right on, what I want to know is who was the pig you laid that right hook on?" Crayon chuckled.

"Yeah, baby. You almost put his coccyx between his balls," Nina smirked, running her thumbs THUNK THUNK THUNK THUNK along the bars of their cell which smelled like it was normally used for a drunk tank.

"I'm really sorry about this, too." Matthew squatted on the concrete floor, propped his elbows on his knees, his bearded chin seated in his palms. He shrugged, stuffed his notebook into his back pocket. Pigs had confiscated the camera, but they didn't discover his notebook . . . . "Listen, Crayon. Nina. Everybody." He turned slowly on his heels until he'd locked eyes momentarily with each woman and man in the cell. "I truly apologize."

"For what, man?"

"For trashing a pig, man?"

"Bullshit!"

"No, listen to me. If I hadn't taken that cop out, then none of you would be in this cell right now. It's because of my lack of control that all of you got busted!"

"Fuck, Matthew, don't you think we can accomplish such feats as this without outside intervention?"

"Oh, I'm sure you can, Crayon. But, we're very likely stuck in this particular cell on this particular night because of one particular lie that this particular hippie told so very long ago.

"You see, man, what you do does come back to you, usually when you least expect it and in ways you never could've predicted."

Crayon leaned down to him, wrapping his arm around Matthew's sloped shoulders. "You really hit that pig like you knew him, man. I mean, you know, like it seemed like a real personal kind of hit?"

"It *was* personal," Matthew stood slowly, staring past milling students to the bone white back wall of the tank.

OFF THE PIGS!
BAIL FOR THE BALEFUL: 666-3333
OR
ESCAPE BY READING INSTRUCTIONS BELOW

Of course, the instructions below had been painted over with battleship gray paint leaving a glossy gray swath where escape once lay. The truth is chiseled on the drunk tank walls. The history of the race. No different from his own. Christ. Couldn't believe his eyes when that baby jowled face leered at him through the glare of the search lights. Covered in a riot helmet, his head looked like a bowling ball. His eyes and mouth were the finger holes. The only thing missing from Emmy Lou's painting: the vestal beasts, facing them down with Billy sticks poised. A bath of blinding white light emanated from spot lights behind their barricades and cordon lines. Just when you think you've got something buried, it appears to haunt you.

The beast broke ranks, rage tearing from his throat like screams of napalmed soldiers, when Matthew popped like a cork on a wave into the front line of demonstrators. The beast's uniform seemed aflame in the lights as he tore through the barricade nearest Matthew, and, swinging his club above his helmeted head, he bore down on Matthew's startled face, also aglow in the blazing lights.

Matthew sensed the charging pig was after him. It was the same kind of feeling he would have when driving down an Interstate and noticing a Smoky in his rearview mirror. Sometimes it caused his Adam's apple to stick in his throat. Sometimes it didn't. But, when he did feel that sudden rush of cold fear, the Smoky would inevitably pull him over. That was what he felt pouring through him as he heard the pig's shrieks shattering the protestors' song.

Flashing boots thudded on the pavement. Matthew recoiled into a crouch, legs flexed like a cat's when ready to spring, arms up in front of his body. Hands, open except for curled fingers, protected his face.

About eight steps away. Seven. Six. A flash of light from a camera in the crowd behind him photographed the contorted screeching baby face. Jesus Christ!

Five steps. Four. Three . . . .

"Donaldson?"

"Parkrow! You creep! Traitor! Stinking commie bastard!" Eddie Donaldson's face looked like a negative as he leaped toward Matthew, sniveling and bludgeoning the air with his Billy stick. "You motherfucker!"

Two steps. One . . . .

Matthew held his ground until Donaldson's stumbling charge brought him to within striking distance. Then, and only then, he leaped to the side and, with the fingers of his hands coiled to make a club of flesh, tore into Donaldson's spine as he fell past him, driving him into the front rows of demonstrators and directly into Crayon and Nina. The blow wasn't a right hook like some had thought they saw.

The cordon lines were sweeping past the barricades with the unblinking yellow lights. The faces of the police were covered with gas masks. Creatures from the Black Lagoon grabbed him by both arms from behind as he attempted to follow the path of Donaldson's fall. They slapped cuffs on him, then hauled Donaldson off toward a medical vehicle. Crayon, Nina, and others who were marching close to them were also snared, cuffed, and led off with Matthew to one of the dozens of paddy wagons lining the curbs of the streets of Chicago.

"I thought I heard you yell his name. And he yelled yours?" Nina sucked on one of Matthew's last Winstons as she leaned forward from her perch behind Crayon on the only cot in the cell. "Didn't you?"

"Come on, Matthew, tell us."

Matthew's lips curled involuntarily. "Wish we had a few good joints to pass around while I tell you this one."

"Tell us the story, man."

"Come on, Matthew, baby, tell us the story about the Chicago pig and you." Nina chucked his bearded face.

Her smile reminded him of how much he had taken. Couldn't he give a little back, too? Even if it was nothing more than a story?

17

"Okay.   Here   goes."   He   lit   a   Winston   which   he periodically waved in the air like a conductor's baton as he recited his story.

Listen my children, and you shall know
Of the trials and treasons of Matthew Parkrow.

He paused to allow for the good-natured groans of the few in the cell who still remembered Longfellow.

It was twenty-one October of sixty-seven--
Most of you who've survived remember
That infamous day as the one
When Amerika charged the Pentagon.

Matthew was confused, on the wrong
Side of the field.
As the battle raged, he knew he'd
Soon yield
To the incessant truth of Amerika's chant:
"All we are saying is give peace a chance."

Somewhere the sun is shining;
Somewhere the sky is blue.
But, there was no joy in Amerika
That day,
For Mighty Peace had struck out.

Matthew lit his final cigarette off of the one he was smoking, which he, then, snuffed on the heel of his sneaker.
"Right on, man!"
"All right, man. All right!"
"Get it on, baby! Get it on!"
"We can dig it!"

At least fifteen bodies huddled closer in the corner of the tank where Matthew paced as he continued his story.

Eddie Donaldson, marked for strife,
Never important in anyone's life,
Was picked to be the man
To spy on the hippies first hand.

Matthew had authored the plan,
So only he could stop Donaldson.
He felt alive again as he charged the line.
He was real once more, getting busted at
The Pentagon.

Somewhere the sun is shining;
Somewhere the sky is blue.
But, there was no joy in Amerika
That day,
For Mighty Peace had struck out.

"Cool it! Turnkey's comin'!"

All the doors were closed to him
Except for those that closed around him.

The guard's boots ceased their hollow thumping. Matthew heard a clanking of metal against metal as a key rattled in the lock to their cell door. "What's this jive-ass shit you're talking, honky freak?"

Matthew wheeled around. Opening the cell door was a slick faced man about twenty-one or two. His taffy face showed nothing of his feelings, if he felt anything. Dull brown eyes looked out at them from smoky whites.

Matthew swept his right hand under his chest as he bowed in the direction of the turnkey and continued his recitation.

So, he turned his mind to newer things
That could not, so soon, drown him.

"What is this shit, honky freak?" Turnkey shoved Matthew and others aside like tree branches blocking his path along a trail as he stepped inside the cell and peered around the tank, seemingly looking for someone.

"Your grace, sir." Matthew groveled on the concrete at Turnkey's feet where the guard's shove had landed him. "Have mercy. I'm just a poor troubadour, a bard of Amerika the beautiful and the home of the grave." He pretended to shudder. Everyone in the tank was in hysterics. "Have mercy, please, massa!"

Turnkey's thread like lips sneered, showing parts of silver fillings in his teeth. "You didn't have none on me." He kicked Matthew's chest with the instep of his boot, pushing him onto his back on the concrete floor and leaning his weight on his foot, thus pinning Matthew helplessly to the floor. "When you was massa!"

The cement was cool through his T-shirt, but Turnkey's heel seemed to brand his chest with fire just over his heart. His heart thudded like kettle drums in the 1812 Overture. Matthew choked out words around short painful breaths from his crushing chest. "I don't . . . don't . . . even . . . know . . . you . . . ." Suddenly, he was seized with coughing and could hardly get his breath at all. He became so desperate for breath that he forced Turnkey's boot from his chest which caused Turnkey to stumble. He grabbed the bars next to the still-ajar cell door. Crayon and Nina immediately knelt over Matthew to protect him. They were joined by four others in the cell who were black.

"Hey, man. You okay?"

"Can you breath now, Matthew?"

Matthew nodded. "VC couldn't kill me. This asshole sure as hell can't," he spit toward Turnkey.

Crayon glared at Turnkey as he straightened himself against the bars and edged toward the door. The demonstrators began creeping toward Turnkey, too, a communal snarl welling in their collective black and white throats. Crayon flashed his hand in the air. "No. Let it be. He's the one who's got to live with what he is." He turned back toward Turnkey, who's face was flushed and sweaty as he slid toward the open cell door. "Better get out of here while you still can, Screw!"

Turnkey bolted through the open door of bars, slammed it shut behind him, and hurriedly locked it. "Christ, you people are crazy!"

"Depends on which side of the line you're on as to who's crazy and who's not." Nina sniveled as she slipped from Matthew's side to the bars near Turnkey. She hugged the bars against her half-bare breasts and flicked her tongue between sulky lips so that the others couldn't see her. "Now me, baby. I'm on the side of your big cock. If you can get me outta here, that is." Her lips parted as she caressed the tips of her teeth with her pink tongue. Turnkey's face beamed despite himself. He straightened, began to strut as he turned to walk back down the scrubbed tile hallway to the cell block door.

"All us white chicks's alike, you dig." She began rattling the bars. "Oh, please! Is it really as big as a telephone pole?"

Everyone in the tank whooped, yelped, crowed, squealed, and banged bars or thumped the graffiti muraled walls.

Matthew struggled to his feet, clinging to Crayon's arm. His chest felt like it was concave over his heart, but Crayon said it was only a bad bruising.

"It'll hurt like hell for a few days, man, but no broken bones or anything."

Trance-like, Matthew began mumbling a new poem as it boiled in his oxygen-starved brain.

Turnkey, oh, Turnkey,
Won't you let me go free?
Turnkey, oh, Turnkey,
Don't you know it's just me?

In the back of the clump of prisoners, a guitar began picking a tune by single notes, then chords, and they all began to sing while they heard Turnkey's scuffling feet hurrying away from them to the cell block door.

Turnkey, oh, Turnkey,
Won't you let me go free?
Turnkey, oh, Turnkey,
Don't you know it's just me?

Whirrrrrr. The block door slammed open. Quick boot steps. Hushed words, echoing inaudibly in the hall. Whirrrrrr. The block door slammed shut.

They told stories and sang songs through the night just as they used to at campfires when they were kids growing up in places like Roanoke Park.

18

When you got nothin',
You got nothin' to lose.
You're invisible, now,
You've got no secrets to conceal . . . .

"I'm so tired, Jason. And, I'm so weary." Matthew searched his father's dead eyes for some sign. "I feel beaten up, you know? I need some real R & R. I need . . . ."
These are the pearls that were his eyes.
"Hell, I only came here because you invited me, you know. Well, didn't you?"
"Christ, son. That was over a year ago. Long before all this." He flailed his arm like a bird in a cross wind. "All of this . . . ah . . . 'mess' you've gotten yourself into."
"Goddamn it, Jason! I've given you the best I've got to offer. We all have. We've given you our courage. We've given you our honor. We've given you our individualism. We've given you our hearts and minds. We've given you our lives, for Christ sake!
"So, we went to Viet-Nam, in spite of ourselves--out of honor and duty to god and country--just like the Boy fucking Scouts of Amerika. Now, parts of us are scattered over those rice paddies and jungles, because you said it was a righteous war.
"Yet, nothing seems to be enough for you. You treat our offerings as if they were gifts from Cain."
"Son. Son. Son. But, when it comes right down to, specifically and only, you--not some abstract 'they' or 'them' or 'your generation', but you--then what are you going to do now with this . . . ah . . . 'mess' hanging over you? And your record?"
"I'm going to teach English, Jason. I just have one semester left until I get my masters degree. That's what I'm going to do specifically now. Teach English."

"And, how long do you think that you'll last at that before you get a hold of some cause or another and get yourself booted out of the teaching profession altogether?"

"Why would you say something like that, Jason?"

"'Cause. Just 'cause." He fidgeted on the end of the couch, as if anticipating what would be a most welcomed interruption by the telephone. "Well, look at your background, your past history, son. Look at your record." Jason leaned forward, counting on his fingers as he began to tick off his list.

"First, there was you not being satisfied with hitting the game-winning home run. No siree, bobwhite! Not my son! No! The Mayor's son had to try and convince the whole world that his home run was really a foul ball.

"Second, you quit the State University baseball team in your junior year even though you were a scholarship All-American second baseman to protest a war you later fought in." Jason wagged his head. "That's one I'll never figure out." He twisted his laced knurled fingers.

"Third, you deserted your military post under combat-like conditions during the Siege of the Pentagon. You, a much-decorated war hero. And you were teaching then!

"Fourth, you've led demonstrations against the very university which was open-minded enough--too damned open-minded if you ask me--to accept you into their graduate school despite your dishonorable discharge and general military disgrace.

"So," he shrugged and reclined into the corner folds of the couch, totally self-satisfied with his presentation of the facts. "Why should I expect anything but your eventual self-destruction as a college English teacher as well?"

A factual deboning, to be sure, Matthew thought. But, he was struck dumb more by how the facts were coming in conflict with reality more and more and more lately than by the factual force of Jason's argument.

The telephone rang. Jason snatched up the receiver. "You're too late, now, goddamn it!" Jason hocked into the

90

receiver behind the barrier of his left hand. "What? Oh, Christ!" He slammed the receiver down. "I've got to run, son. We'll talk more, later. I'm sure we can work something out together."

"But, it's Christmas Eve, for Christ sake, Jason. Can't you get off the political treadmill for just one night?"

"Just a little flap with some environmentalists. Shouldn't take very long. Have Alecia hold our Christmas Eve dinner until eight. Being from the big city and all, I guess you prefer eating late, anyway, don't you?"

"Yes, sir, I do. Maybe we can open presents afterwards by the tree in the living room just like we used to."

"We'll see, son. We'll see. Gotta run, now."

19

Although the meadowlark couldn't fly or stand, it beat tan black-speckled wings, stirring up the snow-like flakes that coated the hole they'd lost so many baseballs in. Claws clutched invisible branches of the loblolly pines leaning over the deep gouge in the earth which Matthew and his friends used as a meeting place before most of the meadows that once surrounded Roanoke Park were seeded by city annexation and sprouted more homes for the home-coming GIs who beat the hell out of Hitler and Mussolini and devastated To Jo and Hirohito. The place where he and Ward and Emmy Lou had often pretended to be cave explorers or pretended they were part of the expedition in *Journey to the Center of the Earth.*

Matthew knelt by the rasping meadowlark flopped on its side, now, eyes glazed and crossed. He shook his fists and screeched at the four crop dusters buzzing Roanoke Park for the third time since he had come out at sunrise to take a long muffled walk in the early morning snow, the first snow he'd seen in a long time. "Goddamn it, what are you doing, you fools? It's Christmas morning, for Christ's sake!"

He scooped up a fist full of accumulating snow. It crumbled like powder in his fingers as he put it to his nose. No real smell, yet a vague almost-scent of some sort of chemical. Deadly perfume. He sniffed it in the gelid air, sensed it clinging to his scraggly beard and collar-length curls and permeating his black-and-yellow flannel CP jacket and his Levis. "You're seeding the fucking snow with poison, for Christ sake." Matthew touched the bird's yellow chest, searching for signs of life. It's wings, now rigid. It's labored breathing, arrested.

Although it was after sunrise, it was not yet light out due to the snow clouds packed in overhead. The crop dusters sputtered and buzzed in the distance. Their sounds seemed muffled in the snow stuffed air. The telephone jangled again past the loblollies. Tears erupted down his cheeks, harlequined by the seeded snow as the meadowlark's stiff cooling body was. Past the pine stand separating the hole from his father's gardener-manicured law, the jangling telephone continued. "What child is this?"

By the twenty-sixth or so time the telephone rang, Matthew's fingers had clawed an opening in the foot of the south wall of the hole where pine saplings bowed to the ground under the weight of the mysterious poison snow which still poured from the clouds. He gathered enough stones to cover the opening after he had nestled the meadowlark in its final resting place. Is that how Ward died in the chopper--arms flapping, mouth gaping, flames consuming his breath, then his body, as, in time, the earth would consume this bird felled by a white Christmas rather than by a VC rocket?

That must be the fortieth call, he guessed. Something was rotten in Roanoke Park and he was--oh shit!--no prince Hamlet nor was he meant to be. More likely the son of Willie and Loch Loaman--the son of the fucking Mayor. Matthew jammed the final stone into the top of the mound of stones now marking the meadowlark's grave. His face screwed against the bitter breeze beginning to swirl the snow around him as he knelt on the floor of the hole, despaired of what to do or say. His field jacket and face were beginning to turn paste white as the snow clung more and more to him. He trembled.

Dead like Ward. Matthew's jeans, too, were spattered white. Like dead Ward. He stumbled to his feet and scrambled hands-over-feet up the clay bank to the pine and honeysuckle thicket where Roanoke Creek now trickled only a hundred feet or so before being diverted by a reinforced concrete cul-de-sac into the sewer at the north end of the hole: a contracting oasis in a desert of VA and FHA housing.

Matthew was nine when his father gave him that Pee Wee Reese four-finger Rawlings PMM. The glove was so big for him that he scooped more sand than baseballs at second base for the Roanoke Park Nomads. Then, Roanoke Creek rushed over a bed of smooth white and gray pebbles and mossy rocks, through the pine woods dense with honeysuckle vines, under an oak bridge where the dirt road shoved a one-car-wide clay gash to the power relay station two miles further into the woods. Thick black cables danced, even then, above the forest canopy to the several isolated settlements just a few miles north of Raleigh. This was the direction things would grow, he'd heard his father say at their dinner table discussions. Jason had encouraged him to ask any questions or to discuss any subject at the dinner table, usually the only time they had together.

"That's why I'm busting my fanny to buy up all this land around us, son." Jason would pull at his stiff white shirt collar, loosen the string tie he wore to ingratiate himself with his rural customers, and puff his chest just a little before he continued in answer to Matthew's persistent dinner table question: What's going to happen to the woods when things grow this way?

"I sell more lightning rods than any salesman in the whole country so I can save this. All of this." He'd swoop his gangly arms in circles as he spoke. "Save it for you, son. Don't you worry none. Nothing's going to happen to your woods, Matthew." He would smile, reach across the blue-and-white checked oil cloth, over the worn Wedgwood platter still containing fried chicken wings and rumple Matthew's hair. "I'll buy it all. I promise, I'll buy it all for you, son."

20

The telephone was ringing again as he crossed the rolling yard which used to extend over a dirt path into a large meadow where the Nomads practiced for their games against the neighborhood teams from other communities at the ends of the other black cables that ran pole to pole from the relay station.

Now, Creek Drive replaced the dirt path. The crab grass meadow beyond had been obliterated by expansions of the original housing development as well as the recent construction of the world's largest ChamCorp distribution plant. When Turkey Locklear first organized the Nomads, there was no field they could call home. The meadow was fine for their practices but the wrong shape for a baseball field.

"We'll play anybody, no madda where or when, long as they got a field!" When Turkey shouted, his Adam's apple bobbed like a turkey when it gobbled, and his voice would break on the high syllables of his deep south accent touched by a year in the Bronx with his birth father when he was ten. "Abner Doubleday invented baseball in a fucking meadow just like ours." That was why Turkey Locklear was their leader. He knew all the impressive information and words you could ever want to know about baseball and owned more baseball cards than anyone else. At thirteen, he was the oldest boy who lived at their end of one black cable. The only one whose voice was changing. The only one who'd had an actual wet dream. And, most important, the only one who'd actually been to New York City, to Yankee Stadium where he had watched his daddy go two for three and a walk with three runs scored and two RBI's to lead the Bronx Bombers to victory over the Chicago White Sox. Turkey's horn rimmed glasses glinted in the sun as they did every time he twisted his head toward his right shoulder just before he threw a curve.

Matthew entered a side door on the northwest side of the house. The door opened directly into Jason's den. It doubled, for all these years, as his office.

"It's aldrin, madam. To destroy those blasted Japanese Beetles, madam. The very ones you've all been complaining about. They would've done to this town what their Zeros did to Pearl Harbor, madam!" Jason Parkrow's swarthy face dripped perspiration as he shouted into the telephone. "I know this is Christmas morning, madam. I have a son whom I still have to play Santa Claus for this morning, myself. That is, if I can ever get off of the telephone, madam!" He pulled at the open collar of his red flannel bathrobe. His matching slippers plopped along the pine-tar colored shag carpet while he paced the length of his new cowhide couch and back continuously as he talked, listened. Suddenly, he flopped his gangly frame onto the couch in mid-stride. He beckoned for Matthew to wait, then whispered into the receiver. "It was an invasion, madam. Our aircraft have been on alert for three days, but this morning was the first morning that it snowed, the first time we could seed the clouds safely. Yes, thank you, madam."

Jason abruptly dropped the copper-trimmed receiver back onto the copper-trimmed base as he leaped from the couch. He stumbled toward Matthew, grabbing his shoulders. "My God, son, you've gotta help get these damned radicals and environmentalist freaks off of my ass! Now that you've given up on all that teaching foolishness or whatever and you've come home, you'll be my number one staff assistant. Your first assignment: Get those fuckers outta my hair, at least what there is left of it."

"What the hell are you talking about, Jason?" Matthew pulled free of his father's grasp. "I never said that I was leaving Columbia or giving up the idea of teaching!" Matthew touched the sore spots left by his father's bruising fingers. "And, I certainly never said that I'd go to work for you. Christ! All those phone calls? Japanese Beetle invasions? Jesus, Jason. Look at my face, will you. My clothes." He sucked in a deep breath. "Look at your hands where you grabbed my shoulders."

Jason tripped back onto the couch as he, first, really noticed his son's end-man face. "What you up to, boy? Imitating Al Jolson?" He forced a quivering grin, ignored Matthew's denial, and lit another Camel, his tenth of the morning already. One still burned in the alabaster ash tray in the middle of the mahogany coffee table in front of the fat couch where he sat. His eyes sought the safety of the Remington hanging from the white oak paneled wall surrounding a shellacked limestone hearth.

The Remington wasn't an original, either. Only a print of *Calvary Charge on a Southern Plain.* Hell, Jason Parkrow, himself, was only a print. That, Matthew reasoned, made him the son of a print. Nothing very original there either. "What are you destroying, now, Jason?" He scowled as he stepped closer to his father's averted face. "I just buried a bird, a meadowlark, in the hole." As he continued, he felt his lips beginning to tremble. He clutched his CP jacket tighter around him as if he were chilled. "That poor bird was covered with the same stuff that I've got all over me. The same stuff that you've got on your hands. Will it drive me insane, then kill me like it did that meadowlark?"

The phone rang.

"Will it, Jason?"

"Mayor Parkrow, here." He lit another Camel from the butt of the one he, then, squashed in the ash tray as he fidgeted in his seat and his face clouded over again. AI have not poisoned Roanoke Park! Quite the contrary, I've saved it from pestilence!" This time he slammed the receiver onto its base. "Goddamned communist bastards!"

"Who, Jason?" Matthew smirked.

"The Audubon Society!" He lit another cigarette, forgetting that he had one burning in the ash tray. "Alecia! Where's my breakfast?"

"Almost ready, yoah honor."

97

From the other end of the ranch-style house, Matthew heard the maid's muffled voice. Maid? Hell. Alecia had been more than that. She'd been his mother, his nanny, his maid, and, quite often, his conscience all wrapped up into one. "The Audubon Society?"

"Yessss! The Audubon Society and the Veterinarian Association and the SPCA and Mrs. Pogowaller across the road. She's helping Naomi Locklear on this bird sanctuary business."

"Mrs. Pogowaller, Jason? That woman wraps flags around her fat ass quicker than mu'u-mu'u's, and she worked that same flag-covered ass off for Nixon just like somebody else in this room did."

Jason tried to smile as the telephone rang again. "You worked for Nixon, son?" he chortled, picking up the receiver. "Why, I'm right surprised at you, son. Hello, Mayor Parkrow, here."

Matthew rose quickly, hoping to escape to the relative safety of the kitchen during this phone call. Jason caught his eye and motioned for him to stay. He sat down again. After all, it was Jason's house. "Japanese Beetles, sir! Is this Adam Gaffendale?" Jason nodded to himself. "Oh, it is. Well, Adam--son of councilman-elected-on-my-coattails-Gaffendale--your goddamned nursery would've looked like fucking Pearl Harbor if my aces hadn't done their jobs this morning!"

"You used Pearl Harbor before," Matthew muttered.

Jason waved him to be quiet. "Thank you. I'll be expecting that token of your support and appreciation in the mail real soon, now." Jason smirked as he spoke. He suddenly seemed to realize the expression on his face and altered it to a Christmas morning Santa Claus smile as he re-cradled the telephone for the umptieth time.

"Son, you heard me say to somebody earlier that I still had a little Santa Claus playing to do myself, didn't you?"

"Yes, Jason. I do believe that, somewhere in the blur of this jingle jangle morning, I heard something like that. I was puzzled then, I must admit. And I'm still puzzled now. I mean, you didn't even get home in time for Christmas Eve dinner after we waited and waited for you."

"Well, son, I am real sorry about Christmas Eve dinner and not opening presents and all that, but . . . ." He pulled an envelop from his robe pocket. "Ho! Ho! Ho!" He shoved the large red envelope at his son. "Merry Christmas, son. Mer-ry Christ-mas!" He waved the envelope in front of Matthew's startled eyes. "Here, son. Take it! This is the best Christmas present anyone could ever hope for."

Matthew did not reach out for the proffered envelope. Instead, he glared at it as if it were possibly booby-trapped. "What is it?"

"Now, that would spoil it. It's a Christmas present, just like I said, son, from ole Saint Nick Jason for you to open and see."

The flap was unsealed as Matthew very hesitantly accepted the envelope with the tips of his fingers, holding it at a distance as if it might be diseased. Opening the flap, Matthew spotted folded typed pages of what appeared to be some kind of legal document. "What the fuck is this, Jason?"

"It's a document setting up a trust of all I own in your name, son. It's all for you, son. It's always been all for you, son.

"The trust will continue to pay all household and estate expenses, and provide for Alecia and Emmy Lou. And, I'll live off of my Mayoral salary and retirement when that time regrettably comes."

"I could never accept this, Jason." Without even extracting the document from the red envelope, Matthew pushed it back at his father.

Jason put his hands up in protest. "No. Everyone's taken care of, son. But, it puts you in charge. Please, son. This is for you. For you like I always promised."

21

"You know that I could never . . . ." Matthew dropped the Trust, unopened, into Jason's lap. "That would be, somehow, like sanctioning what you've done all these years, and I just can't do that. Not now, not ever!" Matthew stomped from the den, through the narrow hallway to the living and dining rooms. There was no talking with Jason, so it seemed. He had his agenda, and there was no reasoning with it or with him. No answers. He took a left into the dining room where Alecia was setting the table for breakfast. Her head was almost cone shaped as if it had been bound by twine when she was a baby the way she'd told him, when he was a small child, that her tribe back in Africa did. Her hair curled close to her scalp like gray wool. Her black lips were like saucers. She'd raised him like her own from the time his mother died at his birth. Jason used to joke that his mother had died of fright after taking one look at him. Jason's jokes might win him votes, but . . . ."

"Lordy, Master Matthew. Wha's dat all over yoah face and coat and look at yoah trousers." She shook her head as she turned from Matthew and the set table and shuffled across the emerald carpet, through the swinging doors into the kitchen.

"I'm playing a reverse Al Jolson in the school play."

"Oh, go on with you now, Master Matthew."

"How long before breakfast, Alecia?"

"Any time, now, Master Matthew. You go on in and wash up first, like a good boy."

"If this shit'll actually wash off. Who knows. I may be permanently stained." He scuffed the carpet until he'd separated the nape enough to see the porous material that the carpet threads were woven through. "Actually, Alecia, the Mayor tried to poison me this morning, I believe." Should serve him the roasted body of that poor dead bird for his breakfast. Bastard! He giggled, however, as he continued. "Tha's why Ah'm sooo white, Ms. Alecia, honey!" he teased.

"Now, Master Matthew, hush yoah mouth!" Alecia slumped back through the pastel green swinging doors, a platter of country ham and redeye gravy in one hand and a large bowl of lumpy grits in the other. Steam swirled from the platter and the bowl as she placed them in the exact center of the Carolina-blue lace table cloth. "Folks is gonna think yoah crazy, Master Matthew."

"Folks already do." He hesitated. "They already do call me crazy, Alecia!"

"Now, Master Matthew," she chuckled, hesitating at the swinging doors. "Why you go and say such a thing." She continued to mumble under her breath as she exited into the kitchen.

Matthew bounced across the carpet, burst through the doors like a gunslinger into a saloon. Eggs were frying in ham grease in a cast iron skillet on the gas stove. The pungent odor of salty ham smothered his senses. Alecia's tiny frame shivered in the kitchen despite the heat. She dropped the butter knife onto the counter top and turned on Matthew. The soft yellow light from the clear dome on the ceiling flattened the lines of her cheeks in shadows of her wide nose. Her eyes were bloodshot like the eggs in the crystal bowl beside the frying pan on the stove waiting for their turn to swim in hot ham grease.

"Goddamn it, Alecia! You have to hatch those eggs to make the hens to lay the eggs to make my breakfast or what?"

"No, yoah honor! Ready right now. Come and get it!" In her shouts, Matthew could not detect even a taint of her frustration. She turned to Matthew and whispered, "Okay, crazy boy." Her lips popped open in a wide smile. "Now off to the bathroom with you a'fore you mess up my whole house and not just my smock."

Matthew glanced at her calico smock, now spotted with white, powdery patches where he had touched her. "Oh, God! You, too, Alecia. That stuff really is poison. I'm not kidding you about that. It killed a meadowlark out by the hole earlier this morning. I buried it in the hole. You'd better change, too."

"Yes. Soon as yoah daddy's eatin'."

She should shake that shit all over his eggs and grits like salt, Matthew thought. Let the Mayor of Roanoke Park eat aldrin.

"You go on, now. I'll save these eggs in the bowl for you."

22

The picture on the midget television compelled Matthew to switch the sound from FM radio back to the television: "Frank Borman, James Lovell, and William Anders are into their ninetieth hour of Apollo Eight, man's first flight to the moon, climaxing, appropriately, on this Christmas day, 1968, with these shots of the lunar surface from the Apollo Eight command module."

The first lunar shots faded to a commercial about letting IBM do your thinking for you. Matthew's leathery skin tingled under a shower of steaming water. The four-inch black-and-white screen above the faucet handles was edged in the same stainless steel which the faucets, the shower nozzle, and the shower door casing were made of. Its screen was protected from moisture and heat by a sealed plexi-glass covering masoned into the walls of ceramic surrounding him except for the door to his left. Until Jason had the television installed last week as the house's Christmas present (he didn't want to miss any of the news just in case he was mentioned), the alternating red-and-white tiles covering the walls and floor had reminded him of a shower stall in the gym at Roanoke Park high school. Jason had it built that way for him when he and his new friend from Florida, Ward Crampton, were the only sophomores to make the high school baseball team in the ten years of the school's existence.

"The astronauts are on the dark side of the moon now. Another American first! So while we are in communications black out with them, we'll go to Jules Bergman at Houston Control for an update on this most recent turn of events right after the following commercial messages."

Marching mechanics filled the screen, singing "Atlantic keeps your car on the go, go, go."

Matthew lathered his scalp and winced when the hot water hit too directly on some of the numerous recurring bumps on his back and arms. Chloracne the doctors were calling it. Jungle rot was all he knew.

"A . . . T . . . L . . . A . . . N . . . T . . . I . . . C . . . . Atlantic is the very best." His lips curled back from his teeth, his face a hideous mask of white paint-like streams and suds spilling from his hair.

It was Ward who made him believe he was a Nellie Fox with power, that the two of them were Tinkers and Evers though their only Chance was a dufuss first baseman they called Stretch because he couldn't. Luckily, they both had strong and accurate arms. They could hit Stretch in the letters most every time so he didn't have to stretch. And, old Stretch did have pretty good hands.

Instead of Jules Bergman's smiling face, film footage of the Pueblo being seized in the Sea of Japan by the North Koreans flashed across the screen. "Eighty-two of the eighty-three-man crew of the U.S.S. Pueblo were released in time to be with their families for Christmas." The Johnny Appleseed like announcer took a deep breath on camera before his beak mouth continued. "Here is a look at some of the happy reunited families on this Christmas morning."

Matthew pushed in the on-off button to the left of the screen, turned off the shower, pulled open the door, and stepped onto the bathroom carpet. Steam hung in the air like the clouds over the earth that brought the poisoned snow. Jason laid the red-and-white indoor-outdoor carpet squares himself after that game-winning grand slam for the State Championship. That way the floor matched the walls, he had explained.

It had been their first game under the lights that year, and they all had trouble hitting until the late innings. They were having trouble picking up the white ball against the backdrop of the lights. Down three to nothing in the bottom of the ninth, Ward started things off with a blooper to right center which he turned into a double with his speed. The clean-up hitter walked. Next at bat was the center fielder, Eddie Mason, who could put one out of the park on his knees when he connected. More often than not, however, he would strike out. There was a hurried confab at the mound between the Capitol City General's coach and his battery. Matthew knew what had to be going on. Walk mason. Load the bases. This guy, Parkrow stings the ball but has less power and he hits left handed against their lefty. Even a base hit with the bases full is better than a home run with two men on base when you're ahead three to zip. Play the ball home for the force out.

Matthew remembered how his stomach knotted up when that lefty pitcher walked Mason intentionally to load the bases. As he dug his left foot deep in the batter's box, Matthew heard his father's shrill voice above the noise of the home crowd. "Smack it, Matthew! Kill the ball, son!"

He concentrated on the pitcher's eyes just like Ward had told him to do. He had concentrated on lefty's eyes once before in the West Side Presbyterian Church parking lot before a dance being held after their football game with the General's last fall. Lefty had been the ring leader of the guys who tried to rape Emmy Lou that night. As lefty began his wind up, Matthew cranked his bat clockwise once, shifted his eyes toward where he knew the ball would be released. He felt sure that lefty also remembered the ass-kicking he had received from Matthew on that fall night. Lefty's blond head twitched towards his pitching shoulder just a little, like Turkey Locklear's used to--dead of lymph gland cancer at seventeen only a week after he'd signed with the Cardinals. Lefty's hand flashed through the glare of lights on the ninety-eight percent humidity hovering in Devereaux Meadow like smog. Matthew cocked his bat at the very last moment. A blur of red stitches tumbled toward home plate. The ball was coming straight at his head. The bastard remembered all right. He was throwing at his head!

Bail out! That had been his instinct. No. Curve ball. It was a roundhouse curve. He was just trying to fake Matthew out, trying to get him to bail out of the batter's box, playing on their past history to make him think the pitch was aimed at his head. Fuck him! Matthew remembered thinking. Stand in tough. Dig back foot in. Begin stride with right foot forward. Commit hips and shoulders but not bat and wrists. It was breaking high. Pull it! Right foot a little more down the line. The blur of stitches was upon him. Commit bat and wrists.

This is for Emmy Lou, you bastard! He didn't feel the concussion of horsehide on thirty-four inches of well-lathed black Duke Snider ash in his clutching fingers, through his forearms, into his shoulders like he expected. As he leaped down the line toward first base, not yet looking at the high line drive sailing for the chain link fence in the right field corner, he wasn't even sure he'd hit the ball except that he'd heard the sound of ball against bat and the roar of the crowd. After he rounded first, he glanced toward the foul pole stretched like a piece of starched tape fifteen feet above the fence. The ball was far above the pole. It seemed to be drifting foul! Goddamn it! He pulled up. Roanoke Park fans in the stands seemed to be applauding, stomping the ivy-choked bleachers surrounding the field on three sides. He started to walk back to the batter's box and pick up his stick when he realized that the ump was waving the ball fair. Somehow, no one else seemed to have seen what he saw in the glaring lights of the ball field. A home run. A grand slam home run. Hot damn! He jogged around the remaining bases and stomped on home plate. Then, he turned and glared murderously at the lefty rapist pitcher as Ward and his team mates mobbed him. But the knots in his stomach wouldn't untie.

As Matthew toweled off, he mumbled to himself. "Even the home team crowd cheered. Ever since Castro had that picture taken on some pitcher's mound in Havana, then took over Cuba as a communist dictator, people in the States had had it in for pitchers. Bay of Pigs, the grand slam that went foul and was called by the umps." He sucked in a deep draught of steamy air. Like a Sai-Gon sauna, for sure.

"You gonna be in there all day, son?" Jason's voice faltered through the mist from beyond the locked bathroom door which had a large color photograph of his game-winning grand slam decapouged on the upper panel. AWe've gotta talk about my . . . ah . . . our . . . ah . . . about your future, son."

Who was he trying to kid? Any talk they would ever really have had already taken place. Anyway, Jason couldn't talk now, or, probably, ever again with his voice so hoarse from all those phone calls. He may even become known as Jason Parkrow, the Mute Mayor.

"Think I'd better just slip the hell out of this place called home," he muttered to himself, "and di di fucking mau back to Manhattan, back to Columbia, back to Emmy Lou's air-conditioned sanity."

How does it feel
To be on your own,
With no direction home,
Like a rolling stone?

Part Three

All things arise from the way

Tao Te Ching

Please allow me to
introduce myself.
I'm a man of
wealth and taste.
I've been around for
a long, long time;
Helped many a man
seal his fate.

"Sympathy for the Devil," Rolling Stones

23

"Please . . . ."

Please allow me to
introduce myself . . . .

"Let me through, please . . . ."

I'm a man of
wealth and taste . . . .

"I'm a medic." Matthew Australian crawled through the crowd. "I must get to the stage right away!" Fat chance that anyone would believe that he was a medic if they got a look at his pupils. But, he repeated the words again and again, anyway, as if he were chanting his mantra. He continued to slide and shove his way through the crowd of three hundred thousand. There wasn't time to explain that, well, he wasn't really a medic, just a Viet-Nam vet who had patched up enough buddies that he figured he might be of some use up there on the stage where all hell seemed to be breaking loose.

When I came home from the fighting, I had a key to our town awaiting me. "From Roanoke Park with love, pride, and devotion to our beloved Matthew in whom we are well pleased." A symbolic key had been wrapped in those words on official Jason Parkrow, Mayor stationery. His key. But, they never actually gave him the real thing.

Matthew worked rock festivals with the Red Cross and in OD tents when he was able. He felt that it was one way to give something back to his people at a time when they really needed it. And, his war experience made him much more calm under the fire of sprains, cuts, overdoses, and the occasional birthing than most "lay" help the volunteer doctors and nurses could get otherwise. Yet, in all those festivals, he'd never seen anything like Altamonte. At least, not since Nam. The vibes were . . . . Christ, the vibes were bad. Like steel bands tightening around his temples. Shit, since before the idea was conceived to have this free concert at the Altamonte Raceway, the anthropomorphization of the idea was doomed.

"Medic! Let me through, please. Medic! Must get to the stage." He parted a couple wrapped in a Navajo blanket. They were simply in the way of his shortest distance between two points as the crow flies, straight ahead, point blank. He wedged between them.

"Hey, fuck off, man," the redheaded boy challenged.

"Yeah, fuck off, man!" his blond companion mimicked.

Matthew felt a warm damp breast and a hard nipple against his left arm as the blanketed couple parted unwillingly like the Red Sea. The dude's prick slapped against Matthew's right thigh like a Billy stick. Jesus! "Christ! I'm sorry," he shouted over his shoulder. "I didn't realize. Sorry!" He fell forward through the next wall of swaying, sweating people.

Inside the acid in his head, flecks of blood were imbedded underneath his fingernails, deep in the quick, as he inserted an oversized "Key to the city" into the lock on the door to Roanoke Park. The dream was always the same, whether in sleep or on acid. When he tried to turn the key, it wouldn't budge. Sirens fractured his stirrups and hammers and anvils like ear aches used to when he was a small child. His father . . . no, Alecia . . . of course, dark comforting Alecia came to him in the night. Her musky odor, sweet like the meadows deep in the pine forests when the meadows were ripe with hay. Alecia. She brought the warm liquid in the square blue bottle. The warm thick liquid which soothed his aching ears. How it quivered his inner bones at first. Then, the heat began to soothe. Within hours, he could hear again without pain. Sirens spit neon words into the sky around him. THIS LOCK HAS BEEN CHANGED TO PROTECT AGAINST TRAITORS! DO NOT ATTEMPT TO USE YOUR KEY TO THE CITY

AGAIN! Matthew dropped the key. Is anyone inside? he asked. This is Matthew. Matthew Parkrow. Son of the fucking mayor. He groped for words, for thoughts. He groped for where the fuck was that voice coming from that spit neon words at him like rockets?

"Excuse me."

"My pleasure, I'm sure," the woman giggled. She winked a volatile violet eye beneath black flowing lashes. Her face was tanned like the rest of her. She stood naked in front of him. A veritable Venus. Her skin breathed. Her face seemed to spread as she pulled him against the hair of her vagina. "Please, baby. Don't run in and out of my sex life like this. Stay awhile with me." She tried to hold him, her vaginal lips pursed for his lips.

"Sorry." He stumbled from her grasp when he saw that head again bouncing around over top of the crowd like a Mitch Miller sing along dot. That was the third time he'd seen that head. "Ward!" he hallucinated that he yelled as he tried to move toward the bouncing dot head. The Purple haze rushed through him like . . . . He wasn't . . . . Was he? Or . . . . The purples and violets in front of him were lines of infra-red photographs of people. Then fluoroscopes of line of people in pulsing purples purples purples purples. Oh, soothe sooth sayer, seer, sayers, Gale . . . smooth delicious violet and the growing, uncontrollable smile. Where going? Somewhere going? Near a stage. To the stage. "Medic!" Help has found its way. "Medic!"

Orange and yellow and red splashed the stage. Jungle drums. Bird calls shook the sound waves. Grunts. Driving piano. Then, Jagger, trying, again, to start *"Sympathy for the Devil."*

Please allow me to
introduce myself.
I'm a man of
wealth and taste.

Lights flashed, flared, and zipped across the sky like tie-dyed lightning. A red-orange-and-black cape dervished about Jagger's lithe body. Matthew noticed separate movement off to the left side of the stage. Nothing more specific. The crowd closed in on Jagger and the stage. The Hell's Angels guards held off about two hundred more from getting onto the stage. The Angels had been beating up on hippies all day long like it was their concert, their stage. What the hell were they doing at the concert, anyway?

I've been around for
a long, long time,
helped many a man
seal his fate . . . .

Rhythm piano and congas counter-pointed his words.

And, there was no one in the town. They had all vanished with the installation of the new lock on the town door. There was . . . only . . . the voice. And, the neon staggering stick men he saw in front of him now, the last line between him and the stage.

"OOOH . . . OOOH! OOOH . . . OOOH! OOOH . . . OOOH!" the crowd cried in rhythm to the music.

The left side of the stage heaved with more motion. Angel's clubs or something else flashed in the white spot lights now beaming down into the crowd. What was that?

"OOOH . . . OOOH! OOOH . . . OOOH! OOOH . . . OOOH!" the crowd moaned.

Matthew couldn't remember at this point how long it had been since the announcement came over the P.A. for doctors on stage.

Suddenly, Jagger interrupted his song. "Cool down!" Instead of singing to his audience, he was yelling at them. "Be cool! Be cool!"

Hell, the Angels weren't being very cool, were they? People in general weren't being very cool, were they? The acid wasn't being too cool either, was it? It was jumping him around inside his own head like a Mexican Jumping Bean in a yerba pod. Suddenly, he covered his eyes with his hands as stage left rippled again with new movement. "Oh, no! It's blades they're flashing." The blades shimmered in the orange light. Music stopped completely. Began again. Stuttered again. Then stopped.

Why had the music died? "Medic! Let me through, please. I'm needed on stage!"

It would be the next day before Matthew would read in the newspapers while on a train to El Paso that the scuffling he'd seen on-stage had been the beginnings of what came to be called the Meredith Hunter stabbing and stomping party held by the Hells Angels. Invitations only.

"Matthew! Wait for me."

He heard the breathless voice somewhere in the void behind him swimming in the humming crumbled wake of his violet and purple waves and the humanity he'd laid waste to get this close to the stage.

"Be cool, Matthew, or those Angels'll stomp the shit outta you."

"Nobody's gonna stomp the shit out of me!" He glared back in the direction of Linda Tallefero's voice. His scowl transformed to smirk. "There's no shit left in me. I haven't eaten in days." Matthew flung his head away from her, his eyes re-riveting on the left side of the stage. Blood. Definitely blood smeared on that Angel's jean jacket covering an embroidered Iron Cross on his lower right sleeve. Damn. He'd forgotten about little Linda until he heard her voice behind him. Rotten luck running into her. She offered to help in the OD tent. Shit, it was just that she didn't want to let him out of her fucking sight once she had found him again. Not with all these foxes running around loose and stoned. Hard to shake her. "Hurry up, goddamn it!" He didn't turn his head back again to see if she'd heard him. Frankly, she gave him the creeps. He plowed on into the sea of sweaty humans all straining to see what was happening on the stage. Why had the music died?

Linda followed, squirming through the crowd toward Matthew who was waving his arms and, intermittently, yelling "Ward" as he pushed through the crowd. She had to admit to herself, if not to him, that she still didn't see any bouncing head that looked like a Mitch Miller sing along dot or a "smiley face" hopping along atop the crowd.

"This sure ain't no Woodstock," a chick to Matthew's left complained to everyone around her and to no one.

"If they'd only consulted astrologer like they did for Woodstock, then they would have found out that today is absolutely the worst day for a concert like this, what with the moon in Scorpio and all. Like that's really heavy, man."

"Hey, that is heavy, man."

"Hell, it ain't been no Woodstock from Santana's set on, man."

Then it hadn't been a whole lot different from what Matthew had expected. Fracases. Minor incidents between the Angels and the hippies. Somebody said the Stones had requested the Hells Angels as security for their concert. No one planning Woodstock would've ever entertained such a thought . . . of giving Angels police-like authority over 300,000 hippies!

"Medic! Medic! Clear the way. Medic coming through!"

It was definitely going to get worse, not better, as the weekend wore on. As best he could, through the violet and purple acid haze he had become accustomed to looking at the world through after being up for about three hours on Purple Haze, Matthew focused his attention totally on the knife flashes and eruptions of blood on the left side of the stage.

24

"What's this shit?"

Matthew heard the scowl in the hoarse voice behind him as he felt a large hand vice-grip his left shoulder in its penetrating fingers.

"A reporter for *"The Voice"* in Chicago? A medic at Altamonte?"

"Oh!" Linda shrieked as she fell over a large man holding Matthew from behind by his shoulders. "Please, don't hurt him. Please, don't." She cowered against his sandaled feet. "Don't hurt us . . . . I'll do anything . . . ."

Matthew felt the fingers digging into his shoulder, then, suddenly, relaxing.

"Oh, miss. I'm terribly sorry. I didn't mean to frighten you. I'm just fucking around with old Matthew, here. We know each other from Chicago. We shared a cell together, didn't we Matthew?"

Matthew knew that voice all right. "Goddamn it, Crayon! You crazy fucker!" He turned and embraced the big dude. "What are you doing here at the end, man?"

"Same as you, I guess, man," Crayon responded as he returned Matthew's hug. "I had to come and see it for myself, you know what I mean, man?"

"Yeah, man. Empirical proof. I know . . . ."

Crayon nodded his head. "I'd hoped that . . . ." He swallowed hard at the words as the two friends pulled apart. "I'd hoped we'd have a little more class than this." He nodded toward the stage and the seeming pitch battle going on up there between Angels and the crowd trying to protect Meredith Hunter. "You know, Matthew?"

"I know, Crayon." Matthew fumbled for a cigarette. "I know, man!" He lit a Winston off of a lighter Crayon offered him. "I'm afraid that it's war on the home front for them that wants it. For the rest . . . . I don't know, man. For the rest of them . . . . Fuck me. I've done my share of the fucking fighting and shit."

"Me too, Matthew. I don't think I can fight still another war . . . . The underground's dying piece by piece . . . scattering out of fear of persecution, man . . . out of fear ."

As they caught up on what had happened to each other since Chicago, they seemed to misplace the purpose for Matthew's desperate attempts at getting to the stage.

"And, what's that on your ass, Crayon?"

"It's a Nixon, man." Crayon spat into his palm and slapped it on the ass patch on his tattered Wranglers. The patch bore a caricature of Richard Milhouse Nixon. "A good likeness, don't you think?"

"Think so, do you?

"Yeah. I do."

"Me too . . . ." Matthew seemed to be gazing off into the encroaching night. "What about Nina, man. What does she think of the patch, man?"

When Crayon grinned, his white teeth seemed to explode across his face. "She also agrees with me. She better, man. She's my old lady now."

"How is she doing?"

"Great. She's in school at Kent State. Wants to be a teacher of kids, you know. Like grade school kids and shit, man."

"Great, man! We need good teachers."

"Dig it! Teach your children well . . . ."

"Right on, man. Right fucking on!" Matthew was trying, with some difficulty, to focus on the conversation. "Ah . . . . When does she graduate?"

"Seventy-one . . . spring semester."

"Cool. You planning to do the marriage thing then?"

Crayon grinned that infectious grin of his. "Yeah, I guess we do."

"That's a long time to wait, man."

"Yeah. But, it'll be worth it." Crayon nodded at Linda. "Your old lady?"

Linda's ears perked up.

Matthew shook his acid head. "No. We just met at Atlanta jam last summer. Just happened to run into each other on the road to this cultural cul-de-sac."

He could at least have lied a little, she fumed to herself. To make her feel a little better . . . to not embarrass her.

"Still hung up on the girl from down home, huh?" Crayon whispered, turning them away from Linda's view.

"Yeah. Emmy Lou. After this cultural joke, I'm on my way to Alamogordo and then to meet her in Denver. I didn't want her here. I was afraid for her safety."

"Same here with Nina. Good thinking as it's turned out, yeah?"

"Yeah. Too damned bad though."

"You know, man, there's this dude in El Paso. He goes by the name of Don Amerika. Runs a gun shop . . . among other things. He can get anything you want or need for your trip into the desert, man, and he's very cool. Crazy but cool. Just tell him I sent you, man."

"Well, I will be going into the desert for awhile, so I will be needing some supplies. Thanks, man.

"And, what does this Don Amerika dude say about your Nixon ass patch?"

"Definitely digs it! Says it's the spitting image of the fucker. Shit, then again, he better think that. He's the one who sold it to me," Crayon cackled. "And, he'll say just about anything to sell you something, man . . . . That's probably his biggest fault."

"Well, it sure goes along with the Nixon ethic, man. And, that's definitely what's 'in' these days."

"Well?"

"Well what?"

"Well, you can't camp out in the desert forever, man. The rangers won't let you. So, what are you going to do after that, man?"

"That's true, man," Matthew laughed. "We'll try Denver for awhile or Boulder . . . or maybe Georgetown up in the mountains. There's lots of hippies around there and in the mountains nearby. We'll just hang out and keep our heads down and our names and pictures out of the papers and off TV for awhile, I guess. I'm going to try to get a teaching job, too."

"Be careful, man. Lots of cowboys out there, too. Not just hippies. Lots of them! Watch out for the cowboys, Matthew!"

"Guess they're just a different version of the Angels." Matthew's eyes rolled for a moment in recollection. "Jesus. That's where I was headed!"

"Where, Matthew? Where?"

"The stage, man. The fucking stage." He tugged at Crayon's gangly frame, trying to somehow pull him along toward the stage with him. "I came here to work the OD tent and Jagger called for doctors or medics a few minutes or a few hours ago. I was on my way to try and help . . . . There's something bad going down on stage. I think the Angels are killing people up there."

"That means getting past those same Hells Angels, man!"

"Guess it does, at that."

"Well, man. I can get you to the stage pretty quick now, but even old Crayon ain't got no pull with them fucking Angels. They've always been out of control, and now that Jagger's given them official status by hiring them as body guards, they're impossible."

"Mick Jagger hired Hell's Angels?" Linda whimpered, still at Crayon's feet.

"Shit, yes!" Crayon looked at Matthew. "Where the hell's this chick been, anyway, man?"

"Obviously not with the Hell's Angels."

"I don't believe that about Mickey!" Her black eyes glazed over as she glared up at Crayon. "How would you know that, anyway, Mister Crayon?"

"Just Crayon . . . ."

"Crayon knows lots of people, Linda. Inside people, if you know what I mean . . . ."

Crayon skinned her alive with his eyes. "Don't believe me! Ask Mick your own fucking self the next time you bump into him over cocktails or something, honey. The revolution's been bumfucked, honey . . . by you, by me, by Matthew, and by everyone here at this race track including, and most especially, Mick fucking Jagger!"

Linda felt her bottom jaw drop, and she couldn't seem to take up the slack. What an asshole . . . . Matthew, too . . . . Matthew, too, hell. Matthew most of fucking all.

"Come on, Matthew. This way to the stage, man."

Crayon hugged Matthew's slender shoulders with his huge left arm, pulling him through the crowds like a rag doll, away from Linda and toward the Hells Angels. As people in the crowd noticed Crayon, they automatically moved aside for one of their most recognized leaders.

Linda did not try to follow Matthew. She wasn't going to do that any longer. Serape or no serape, you could bet your ass on that! She turned in the swarm of humanity choking the Race Track infield and stalked away from the Meredith Hunter knifing that was still taking place on the stage.

Why ask who killed
the Kennedys,
when, after all, it
was you and me . . . .

Knives again flashed in the flood lights. "We'd better hurry, Crayon!" So, it must have been Crayon's head he saw bouncing around on the shoulders of the audience earlier. Not Ward's. No Ward in New York. No Ward in Chicago. And, now, No Ward at the end of the fucking world being staged at the Altamonte Race Track. There must be no more Ward Crampton anywhere. Blown to bits in a helicopter in Viet-Nam. R I P . . . .

"OOOH . . . OOOH! OOOH . . . OOOH! OOOH . . . OOOH!"

25

"WOOH . . . WOOH! WOOH . . . WOOH! WOOH . . .WOOH!"

A train whistled in the distance. It sounded like a city version of a coyote's howl. Matthew thought that it could easily be the same train he had arrived on only an hour before he faced racks of rifles jamming the pine paneled walls of Don Amerika's Gunshop.

The glass storefront bore the shop's name in dayglow red, white, and blue matching the American flag carpet. Every seven feet in each direction a stars-and-stripes stood out against the basic uranium gray of the carpet. Standing behind each flag was a life-size fiberglass figure--Jesse James, Wild Bill Hickock, Buffalo Bill Cody, Pat Garret, Davey Crocket, Daniel Boone, William Travis, Sam Houston, Steven Austin, James Bowie, J. Frank Dobie, Frank Robinson, Dwight David Eisenhower, Chester Nimitz. Each figure displayed a glass-and-aluminum case in its belly, locked with a polished Yale lock and containing certain specialties of the shop such as Seiko watches with compasses, hollow point shells, and western style pistols. Beyond these figures, a triumvirate displayed shelves of various caliber cartridges in their bellies. Lyndon Baines Johnson, Katharine Ann Porter on each end and Richard Milhouse Nixon in the center, his hands reaching out to bless the adjacent NCR register. A fourth figure lurking just behind the register was arrayed in a Captain America costume. But, the Captain America figure had no display case in its belly. And, its arms, legs, and head began to move, turning toward Matthew. It spoke.

"Hey, man."

Matthew stared hard at the statue that moved and talked as it sauntered from behind the cash register between Crocket, Boone, Travis, and Austin toward the statue closest to the entrance near Matthew, Chester Nimitz. His name, as all the others, was engraved in bronze on a slave necklace locked around his neck: Don Amerika. He offered his wrinkled hand. "Don Amerika. This is my shop. Need something to shoot?" he giggled. "And these . . . ." He waved his arms about, seeming to indicate the figures. "And, these are my creations."

"Hey, man, that's cool!" Matthew grasped the wrinkled hand in his, expecting it to be weak and fragile but finding instead a sturdy grip. "I'm Matthew. Crayon from Berkeley recommended your shop, man."

"Hey, that's cool, man. Crayon is a righteous dude, man, a real righteous dude! So, welcome, then, Matthew, friend of Crayon's. My place is yours, man."

"Are you for real, man, with this get-up and," Matthew swept his arms indicating the entire store, "and this place?"

"Hey, Matthew, man." He shrugged and leaned against Nimitz. "You gotta survive, man. Like everything's gonna start coming down real heavy, you know, man . . . like real soon . . . . For freaks, you know, like you and me, man, it's gonna be a real 'freak out'!"

"You're probably right, Don. But, right now, I'm heading out into the desert. I need a few things, Don . . . like a rifle . . . rounds . . . ." He chuckled. "A horse . . . ."

"The horse you'll have to get from Hickock's livery across the street. I don't deal in horses. But, I can help you with the rest. Come on back, man. Let me show you what I've got, man."

As he followed Don Amerika towards the back of the shop, he saw Don disappear behind Katharine Ann Porter. A metal door screeched on its hinges and scraped the concrete floor behind the counter as it opened. The door slammed shut. Don's boots clomped across the cement floor. The silence.

"For the rattlesnakes of all kinds out there, man." Don winked his gloucous eyes like pieces of atomic glass in the sand as he emerged from behind Katharine Ann Porter. His arms spilled over with a Winchester, six boxes of thirty-thirty shells, and a matchbox he said contained one hit of organic mescaline and about fifteen grams of golden smoking powder.

"Wow, man. This is perfect!"

"We aim to please, man." Don's eyes, rather than penetrating, seemed to surround Matthew, sucking him up.

"How much?"

"For a friend of Crayon's, man? Let's say seventy-five even." Captain Amerika hesitated, cracked his knuckles. "The rifle's hot . . . from Morocco. So . . . ." Don Amerika shrugged his shoulders again. "You pays your money, and you takes your chances, man . . . . Say . . . one fifty for the whole stash . . . ."

"Okay, man. Sounds good to me." Matthew paid him from the clip in his left front pocket.

"If you like the merchandise, man, let me know. I've got a very cool connection there."

"Where?"

"Morocco, man. Morocco. I can get you guns, dope . . . the best black hash . . . Lebanese blonde the color of a monk's robe."

"Cool, man."

"So . . . you really are going into the desert, man?"

Matthew nodded.

"What the fuck for, man. Ain't nothing in the desert but sand and sidewinders . . . and ghosts . . . all kinds of fucking ghosts, man."

"What else does a guy do with an MA in literature?"

"MA in lit, huh?"

"Yeah. Just finished my thesis defense a few weeks ago . . . or was it a few years ago? Can't keep time straight anymore."

"I know what you mean."

They both chuckled.

"Lots of pilgrims used to pass through here, man, on their way over the Franklin Mountains to Alamogordo." When he finally asked Matthew if he was looking for the cradle endlessly rocking, too, like those other pilgrims,

Matthew snatched up his packages and the rifle and flung himself past Bowie, Crocket, Houston, Nimitz, out through the remote-controlled doors without even saying good-bye or thanks.

Don's square soft face hollered after him as he fled to his rented jeep. "Happiness is black hash, man. Happiness is a Lebanese Blonde, man. Happiness is a warm gun from Morocco, man!"

Part Four

*Be at one with the dust
of the earth*

Tao Te Ching

26

GODZO.

Matthew started from a nap in the saddle as sand-blasted planks creaked on nails in the wind blowing up from Mexico. There was rain in the clouds scattering from twin mesas in the east toward the sun. He squinted at the crumbling placard tacked to a fir framing stud driven into the sand by a workman twenty-four years before. Matthew reined in the bay quarter horse from Hickock's Livery. It snorted and pranced beneath him. He dismounted and led the gelding toward the padlocked gate in front of the sign, the only entrance through the jagged link fence surrounding what was left of Project Manhattan.

GODZO.

The other letters sand covered. The parched stud was splintering in the center from the years of pelting sand. Staleness of the rain not falling swept past on another gust from the southwest.

GODZO.

From below the Rio Grande, you could almost smell the enchiladas stuffed with chunks of chicken still clinging to the bone. Slamming kitchen doors, the wind whirled north toward Gallup. The bay pawed at scrub grass growing around the edges of the fence that squeaked like prairie dogs. Matthew buttoned his denim jacket over his work shirt. Inside his jeans' watch pocket, his left hand discovered a coiled strand of leather. He pulled it out, pushed back his black curls as they flopped in the wind, and tied the leather strip around his head. After tethering the horse to his left ankle, Matthew squatted in front of the corroding lock. He brushed graphite-like dust from around the tumbler. A sunburst of gouges surrounded it like the Military Intelligence insignia, like his court martial. With the Swiss Army knife he had carried since he took his first oath as a Cub scout, he jimmied the lock in a matter of seconds. That it had been forced before--many times before--made it that much easier. In fact, he was a little surprised that the gate was locked at all after all this time. He shoved the gate inward, untethered the bay and led him through.

"Cheeh, boy. Come on, boy." Desert wind, dry as the sand it whirled at the wooden sign, howled. No rain left in the clouds after all.

Now that the sand was blowing off, he could read the words they had printed all those years ago . . . .

GROUND ZERO.

Oppie Openheimer had code name it Trinity.

"So, this is where we were born?" Matthew turned, closed the gate, slid the open lock back into place. "We could've all been blown to hell that day. Instead, it was merely another explosion, only it was eight thousand feet up and five thousand two hundred and eighty feet out." Under the green mushroom, Oppenheimer, Bainbridge, Kistiskowsky, and Greisen shrieked the *'Los Alamos Blues,'* leaped in primordial dances celebrating the fires of hell they had just vitiated the desert morning darkness with. Four weeks later, eyes dribbled from sockets, singeing stunned cheeks in Hiroshima . . . the Nagasaki.

"Easy, boy . . . easy now." Matthew stroked the fidgeting gelding's neck as they approached the disintegrating skeleton of an outhouse sprawled on its side near the observation blockhouse. "No dancers celebrating our birth today, huh boy? Just you and me and that armadillo over there. While we were waiting to go to the Nam, we used to chase them on the tank course at Fort Hood, flying across the prairie in front of a rooster trail of dust. When you got real close to one, it would roll up into a ball." Nothing else to do but get ripped and play softball with armadillos at night in the spring. Waiting . . . .

The armadillo scurried through scrub brush behind the outhouse towards four eroding concrete pillars which had once held the steel tower where the throbbing prick had dangled above cunt earth. A shudder in the loins engenders there the broken wall, the burning roof and tower and Agamemnon dead. The antelope fled. No armadillos squealed. No prairie dogs scurried. No rattlers rattled.

Matthew untied the reins and lashed them to the outhouse door hinges. The door itself was gone. All the doors were gone: in the ranch house, in the outhouse, in the blockhouse, in the Skinner maze instrument bunkers.

Just like it said in *Esquire*: *"Alamogordo, Mon Amour."* The twentieth century Gordian knot, its doors torn from their hinges for souvenirs or firewood when, surrounded by incense of memories, the yearly pilgrims gathered on the Sunday nearest July 16 to commemorate the creation of their age. Gallup had reported tremors and windows rattling like snake tails that day. Cordoned off by Army evacuation forces in case the wind shifted during the test, Carrizozo, a town unaware of its real peril, thought the judgement day was at hand. Thousands applied to Bombshelter, Inc. They would pioneer a new market. Millions flocked to the churches. The churches said: "A million American lives were saved. Praise God! From whom all blessings flow." Still confused from Hiroshima and numb from Nagasaki, the Japanese surrendered on the U.S.S. Missouri. General MacArthur's voice broke: "These proceedings are completed." The pilgrims bowed their heads: "Praise God! From whom all blessings flow . . . ."

Sand swirled as Matthew pulled the leather strap slowly through the lockloops. Opening the left saddlebag was like opening a time capsule fashioned out of fresh cowhide. In the bag, his left hand felt the rough sides enclosing six cartridge boxes, a six-inch iron skillet, one box of Ohio Blue Tip matches, a ballpoint pen, his journal, the most recent *Rolling Stone* he'd picked up at the train station, a new Rand McNally atlas he'd lifted from his father's Continental before sneaking off without eating breakfast or saying good-bye last Christmas, an aerial photo map of the missile range and adjacent areas he had salvaged from his aborted military days, a small match box holding his stash, his crisp new parchment attesting to the world his mastery over literature, and some fuzzy thick rope. Hobbles.

"I'll need some hobbles for that horse you rented me," he reminded the hardware salesman in Hickock's Livery & Hardware two blocks north of Don Amerika's Gun Shop. Hickock squinted at him from under scar tissue lumped over his dull green eyes like make-up putty as he stacked gallon cans of Spread Satin outside white.

"For your hoss, hoss?" His words poured down steel chutes into forms for driveways, sidewalks, patios overlooking the vast desert beauty. "Don't carry such ready-tied. He scratched his bald head as if he had a full head of hair growing on it. "Got some good, strong rope though. You can tie 'em yourself. The hobbles." While he muttered, he walked to the end of the plywood paint counter in the rear of the creaking wood store, extracted a spool of rope from the top shelf behind the counter and lugged it back to where Matthew was popping his knuckles, waiting. "I'll show you how to tie 'em, hoss. Used to be a mustanger myself . . . tied millions of 'em . . . ." As an afterthought he added. "No charge, of course, for the lesson."

As Hickock smiled, Matthew stared at his withered gums. The boxer once. Turpentine and nails and rope remained to remind him every day of that red sash once girded around his head, a sword swishing the air in his right hand. Some have been bred down in the hips so much for show that they can bear pups only through cesarean section. Dysphasia. Or bulldogs. Some dogs tenacious. Probably got his windpipe busted a few times as well as his African elephant ears. Matthew nodded again or had he nodded the first time? He did not, anyway, paid Picasso of the hobbles for the rope and left, both of them shaking their heads as one thought about the other. Imagine, Hickock thinking that Matthew--with all his experience at playing cowboy while growing up in Roanoke Park--would need lessons in how to tie hobbles.

Matthew hobbled the bay's front legs, fed him a few cubes of sugar fetched from his denim jacket pockets. "Be easy, fella. It's just the wind." The bay whinnied, then stood quiet, munching the sugar cubes. The wind was voices. Voices of the pilgrims: "Praise him all creatures here below . . . ."

"Be back soon, fella." Matthew patted the horses neck. His boots squeaked in the sand as he followed the armadillo's path through the scrub brush to where the twenty-five-foot cunt lay covered by billowing sand under the hundred-foot steel tower that vanished in the fireball. Bites of trinitite nestled in sand like emeralds in a thief's hand, the remaining evidence of that conflagration. At twenty-four, the crater still bore the stretch marks of the rough beast born out of its belly and of the many pilgrims, some of whom had left a generator propped against one of the pillars, a rusting sacrifice: "May the Lord bless you and keep you and make his face to shine upon you . . . ." A chill in the dry rot wind, then olfactory vacuum.

The rain clouds had passed with the shifting of the wind. Now, they were streaming across the sun, wound red and sliding toward Japan. It would soon be too dark to make camp. He knew he had to get out of White Sands before dark. The area was still sometimes patrolled at night. Couldn't stay anyway. Probably still a little hot even after all those years had passed. If one-eighth of the radiation was still left as the third half-life began, then was that enough to do humans damage? Should've brought a slide rule, a protractor, a Geiger counter, a calculator. Excalibre.

27

Matthew could still see the sculptured hollows that were Don Amerika's cheeks, the cascading yellow hair that was his neck, the Captain America outfit that was his skin while he rode his quarter horse across the desert away from the sunset and chain link fence toward the twin buttes two miles north of imploded concrete dugouts which surrounded the perimeter of GROUND ZERO. The soiled Winchester slung on the right side of his saddle bumped in two-four time in its rawhide sheath as the bay galloped through wild sand in their faces. When the first shock waves shot across the desert, a herd of antelope, grazing on those buttes, had vanished in a crazed stampede into Mexico. Desert shifted to prairie, advancing toward the Sacramento Mountains.

Receding, Trinity and the wrecked rigging tower, a sculpture twisted from three hundred feet of melting steel hunched against the earth like a person worshipping or cowering. Spattered about the blackened tower, eruptions of blood brown dirt. Headless observers. Tomorrow he'd try to wangle a closer look at those silos towering to the south like tusks in an elephant grave yard, a place bulging with fruit from this withering harvest. But, they don't like us to know we've become strontium 90. Beta. Cesium 137. Cobalt 60. Europium 152. Gamma. Jade air absent of smell with a musty texture.

The pilgrim wind: "God our help in ages past, our hope for years to come, our shelter from the stormy blast."

Deceiver.

"Remember the rickety wooden guard tower at the rear of the compound on Pham Nu Lau Street, how it would sway in the monsoon winds blowing the moon from Sai-Gon toward Burma? How we always hoped for rain during our guard?" He patted the horses' flank. Rain seemed to keep the mosquitoes grounded in the saw grass marshes that strangled the banks of the tributary of the Sai-Gon River running under the Bien Hoa bridge.

"It's time for you to drive Ward to the airstrip." Sergeant Smiley's frog voice echoed off of the low panel walls which divided the stone warehouse into offices.

Ward Who? Ward flying into the Iron Triangle. Ward: chopper downed beyond our outer perimeter. Four guards saw the fireball of the crash. Ward Crampton: MIA. Presumed dead. Everything a blur . . . b.

"Of course you don't remember, nameless horse." Matthew clucked his tongue. The bay dug his rear hooves into the crumbling sandstone slope and scrambled up, over a low ledge onto the top of twin mesas. Where the antelope once played seemed to have been ravished by rhinos, napalm, white phosphorous, aldrin. No. None of these left a fine red powder. Oxidation: only the rust of years. In the center of this southernmost of the two mesas, a semi-circle of smutty stones squatted like an altar scorched from sacrifice. Someone had camped here before, many times before.

Won't get much of a fire going, though. Not a damn thing to burn out here but sage and radioactive outhouse planks. The sage burns too fast. Be lucky if I can cook my eggs while I try to keep warm in the serape Linda gave me.

Matthew touched his right saddlebag. Hope none of the eggs have been broken. Be a mess in there if they did. He dismounted a few feet from the foot-high crescent of rocks built against the prevailing winds from below Carlsbad Caverns and hobbled the bay.

"Got to scrounge something up for a fire, boy." Reaching behind his saddlebags and bedroll which were lashed behind the unscrolled, oildarkened saddle, he untied the burlap feed bag.

"This is the last of the oats, fella." Matthew whispered while he fit the bag over the gelding's mouth and behind his ears. Bet Buzz Aldrin built a great fireplace after he collected his forty-eight-and-a-half pounds of dirt and rocks from the moon. He was flying around up there just anticipating the hell out of that landing. But, there's no wood on the moon either.

"Eat 'em up, fella. We'll both be living off of sugar and water by tomorrow unless we run up on some indigenous supplies . . . ."

28

Matthew struggled under an armload of split logs. He had found a cache under a ledge at the far end of the butte which must have been left by some previous pilgrim. "Hardwood firewood . . . ." Matthew wagged his shaggy head, the black curls falling over his denim-covered shoulders, muttering to the wind. "Out here in the middle of the desert . . . ." Must be somebody's main camp, he inferred. He reeled across the mesa top to where the bay stood, munching oats. He stumbled the few steps further to the rock pile and dumped the wood into the red dust beside them.

Maybe, like Colonel Flanger had warned, THEY are trailing me. Could that be true? Haven't felt really free since I was kicked out of the Army. No. No fresh ashes. No fresh tracks. Don Amerika was right about that spying shit, though. THEY want you to look under your bed and in your closets every night, before you retire, for communists. And, I do look every night, but for bugs . . . and I don't mean bed bugs or moths either. Maybe I should check out the sage brush and cacti, too.

The purple sky was cloudless now as his gray eyes pierced the twilight. In the west, the shrunken site appeared to be exactly what it was: White Sands Missile Range. As Matthew constructed a teepee of three logs over sagebrush and wood chips, he shivered. Even cold as it gets at night, this pile ought to be enough. He shoved more sage underneath the teepee and struck an Ohio Blue Tip with his thumbnail. He pushed its yellow flame into the sagebrush. The brush crackled and flared toward the sky where a few stars were beginning to cluster near Mercury. The communion wafer moon was climbing from behind the eastern horizon. The dry timber caught quickly. Sparks floated into the darkness of the adjoining butte: fireflies.

Matthew scrambled eggs with his knife as they firmed at the edges in his iron skillet. The last of the dozen he'd bought from a Pueblo farmer the morning before. Soured a little in the heat of the saddlebags and the plastic bag which held them cradled and cushioned in Linda's serape. The quarter horse snorted, tried to paw at the sandstone ridge with hobbled hooves.

Something in the wind. He senses it. Upwind, Matthew thought that he heard a coyote howl . . . . No. None left out there. We did save millions of cows from their ravenous jaws by tempting them with strychnine baits until there were none left to tempt. Now scientists study their sacred-cow children that witnessed the blast for signs of radioactivity like Ward and I studied the five-legged black Brahma bull near Kuala Lumpur.

We searched for stitches, graft scars, anything. There weren't any. Only a fifth leg, its hoof flopping alongside the Brahma's velvet hump. Brown skin showed in spots where the mutation had rubbed hair from the hump as the Brahma, pulling always at his leather tether, stomped in a muddy circle below the thousand-and-one crumbling stone steps hand cut into the mountain which led to the caves of darkness and light.

The dark cave, they say, runs from Malaysia to Thailand. Many have tried it only to never be heard from again, so the legends go. In the light cave: all those gods encased in glass. Couldn't take a photo without too much glare except where the cave's ceiling ruptured into a twenty-five-foot gash of topaz sky. The only vegetation in the cave was the ferns drooping from that hole towards the sandy floor and one sapling stretching from the rupture toward the ferns and the sun.

"The girls say we have to get back to town now if we're gonna make our R&R flight to Sai-Gon, Matthew."

Seven days. Where had they gone? "Yeah, Ward. I'm coming." Matthew had snapped one last shot of a black figurine almost directly under the hole in the cave ceiling: god of fire and pestilence. Then, he shuffled across the sandy floor toward the luminous mouth of the cave where

Ward was already helping their lovers for the week down the first of the mountain's thousand steps.

Tanya, Ward's girl, was from Morocco originally, and she was saying as Matthew approached: "Ward, if you ever be in Marrakech, go see my brother there. I give you name, address before you leave. He take good care of you if you say you know Tanya."

"Okay," Ward had chuckled, "but tell him not to hold his breath until he hears from me. Okay?"

Matthew had laughed with them as he caught up with them on about step nine-hundred-and-ninety and descending. The girls seemed puzzled by these crazy GIs who laughed on their way back to war.

After the blast at Alamogordo, nothing was left for over a mile. The towering steel pelvis disintegrated like that outhouse had, only its dissolving was instantaneous when its penis rammed home. Matthew pulled the pan from the fire as the eggs bubbled and hardened, almost too much.

After the stabbing at Altamonte, there had been nothing much left either. He balanced the pan on the edge of the rocks and stumbled through flickering light and shadows being woven by the fire as if they were on a loom to where his saddle sprawled in the red dust covering the only rock ledge to the east. Suddenly, he felt chilled. In his right saddle bag he located the serape . . . silver-and-turquoise thunderbirds decorating it . . . given to him by that eighteen-year-old vamp from Memphis.

"If I can't keep you here with me," Linda had whimpered while smothering him with her olive flesh, "then at least you won't forget me when you're wearing my favorite serape from Leon."

It had only been three weeks since Atlanta jam when he gave in to her entreaties and visited her in Memphis . . . not exactly a longhair's city . . . only four weeks since his orals at Columbia. He had met Linda Tallefero in the medical tent at the jam. That was fate. That he visited her in Memphis was a mistake. Matthew wrapped the serape around his shoulders as he shuffled back to the spark spitting fire.

Eggs okay. Could've called him Ishmael if she'd conned him into marrying her. Atlanta Jam could've been Atlanta crazy glue with his Egyptian vamp from Memphis who swore that computers could write books.

"You don't have to go to that place to write about it," she said, and maybe she was right. It was all mathematics anyway. Language: metaphorical mathematics.

"You're living in a dream of individuality, Matthew. Hot cunts and fast computers . . . that's where it's at, baby!" Her writhing body almost burned him, it was so hot as she squeezed him clean with a grunt and a smile.

"Can't you stay with me, Matthew, and keep my honey pot boiling? Please?"

The artist's tools become the computer program. Instead of apprentices or researchers, the new creator will have PC Jr. The mainframe must be reserved for bank billings and graves registration where they are sorely needed. Without their mainframes, utilities would probably send out bills later and charge less. With the artificial intelligence chips of the future, we will be closer than ever to approaching the anthropomorphization of thought. If we reduce everything knowable to ones and zeroes, then there's simply nothing we can't understand, now is there?

Look, for instance, at our relationship with GODZO. Like a father. Shot up my mother, filled her to obesity with births where the secret mewls and pisses pictureless sensations: mass moves above; heat blows glaring noises.

Matthew popped the fork attachment out of his knife and wolfed the eggs from the still-sizzling skillet in six steaming slurps. Hummm. Pungent eggs ala campfire. An appropriate birthday dinner.

The bay was kneeling, asleep. The moon was a phosphorous scythe dangling over Trinity. "To the day the music died!" Matthew lit a joint and lifted it up as if toasting with a glass of wine. He sucked in a deep choking

137

hit and held it in his lungs. His nostrils snorted to keep the breath and the smoke in. He felt the rush. Exhaled slowly.

"To the day the music died!" Crayon had snorted. "To Altamonte!" they had shouted together. His memory of that last toast with Crayon seemed as real inside the campfire as it was when it actually happened three days earlier. Somehow it seemed as if much more time had passed than that.

"To the day the music died!" Matthew placed the mescaline tab on the back of his tongue. He could feel it beginning to dissolve even before he was able to take a swig of tepid canteen water. He drank the water anyway, washing what was left of the tab down his throat cleanly.

Just over twenty-four years before, President Harry S. Truman received a coded message at the Potsdam Conference:

Babies satisfactorily born.

Fat Man . . . . Little Boy . . . .
GODZO.
Nothing moved.

29

Matthew couldn't be sure what roused him from his trance. That jet crashing the sound barrier or the noiseless steps he sensed shuffling through the red dust near his campfire. Now, it was only glowing coals. The cinders were cities crumbling and new ones rising from their ashes. Maybe, it was the mescaline finally kicking in. He'd been sitting for hours just staring at fiery masks. They glared at him from the fire. Next to them in the night, the silhouette of a hunched figure, slumped cross-legged in the mesa dust with hands outstretched over the dying embers. A faint stench permeated the otherwise clear desert air. It was a smell Matthew knew but couldn't recall what it was.

Jason? Sorry, I left without us having that talk you wanted or even saying good-bye. No. How can I be sorry for the inevitable. You even said that much yourself.

The stench grew stronger as Matthew continued to feign sleep, trying to place that smell. His right hand crept from under the blanket wrapped around him. Fingers groped until they touched the linseed-oiled stock of his Winchester. He had seen Ward somewhere in a desert like himself. His hand eased the rifle from the case and lifted it onto his blanket.

Remember. Flip the fucking safety off before going for the lever. These people are capable of anything. Fathers. Not the least of which is that they produce sons like me: personifications of the Cartesian dichotomy. Wellstones and the water they enclose. I am a wellstone. My spirit is the tanictinctured water oozing through my panicpunctured walls like White Water Bay in the Everglades spills through cypress into the Gulf of Mexico. Careful! Fathers are the wellripping roots.

"Won't be a'needin' that, sonny." The shade's words crackled like dry lightning. Crouched by the fire, it turned from its waist, peering past what was left of the flames through the night. Out of the fireflush, eyebrows leaped like whiskbrooms from the figure's brow. Its disheveled beard cascaded down its chest like clumps of sheared wool. The stench was becoming overwhelming. The shade's clothing seemed to smoke as if about to catch fire.

"Don't mean ya no harm, sonny." The words still crackled. He backed away from the heat patting himself all over to quell the almost fires in his clothing. "A little too close to the fire. You do that sometimes if you can't see, you know, sonny."

How did any man hear him going after his rifle? He made no sound? "Who the hell are you?" he heard his voice say with a strong tinge of protecting his territory as he stared at where the figure's eyes should've been gleaming in firelight. The old man's were flatblack holes. There was no gleaming in the firelight. The stench gradually dissipated into the snappy desert air.

Beyond the old man, a puma hissed. Snap. Matthew flipped off the Winchester's safety. Clickclack filled the rifle chamber with a round. When he bolted up, the army blanket fell from his shoulders. All he needed was a dead fucking horse. He aimed from the shoulder toward the increasing hisses.

"No!"

Matthew gaped as the old man struggled to his feet, blotting out the golden crescent moon that still floated through clouds over project Manhattan behind him. It had only been days since Buzz Aldrin walked on that surface. Occasional slivers of moonlight flashed off the chain link fence in the distance and danced along the old man's shoulders like St. Elmo's Fire through a schooner's rigging. "That's my puma. She ain't gonna hurt ya either, sonny."

Matthew dropped his aim momentarily, but he did not relax. Maybe this old man was one of THEM. "Who are you?"

"I'm the one what knows the truth. I'm the only one what saw it!" He grinned and shook his head. "Poor old Estevan."

"Hell, we've all thought that before."

The old man did not speak.

"Okay, old man, what truth?"

"The truth!" Estevan stabbed at the blackness above his head with withered hands. The puma's fangs suddenly gleamed in the firelight from the shadows behind his knee. She hissed. "Quiet, No-cat. Quiet!"

Although Matthew could see only shadows of the cat's front haunches, he could tell from the level of its chartreuse eye slits that it was still sitting like a dog behind its master's left heel. The rifle slid from Matthew's loosening fingers onto the army blanket bedroll bunched up around his hips. "The truth? The truth? What the hell is the truth, old man?"

"I'm the only one what knows it. Poor old Estevan. The only one what saw it! Poor, blind Estevan." He stomped up dust with rag wrapped boots. "That's how I got blinded!" His dried fig fingers clawed at empty sockets. He slumped again to the ground, red dust splashing over him and faced the fire. No-cat slouched into the darkness beyond the firelight's reach. "The truth blinded me."

Matthew's horse snorted and pawed at the stone ledge where he stood, hobbled. A night hawk bolted for the moon. Its wings thrashed ancient desert air. Old as Daedelus . . . Icarus. Old as the envy swelling in Matthew while he followed the black dot as it streaked past the yellow crescent into the darkness yawning out of his reality. DiVinci knew their quest. He drew fliers patterned after what he observed in birds. If we peel the secret like rings from a tree, we'll be able to fly, the right brothers had, finally, to think before they could command a concrete pylon erection on Kill Devil Hill because they had flown the first time with power of their own driving those wooden wings into the outer banks wind. Wright on!

Blasts of thunder echoed over the mesa from somewhere near White Sands. "Damn, that jet sounds like the Saturn rocket taking off, you know?" he muttered. Buzz Aldrin flies through space in Apollo and aldrin snow flakes permanently ground a meadowlark in Roanoke Park.

Estevan, startled from his stupor-like infatuation with the heat of the flames from new wood Matthew had placed on the fire as he sat beside him, grunted in response, then retreated further into his meditation. Jests and jets were nothing new to the uranium prospector. Jests were his nightmares where he could still see with his own eyes, not just through the eyes of No-cat and Jackass. Jets, they were the condors of his visions, forever tearing at his eyes. Already a memory fading, the afterburner roar of the jet seemed to hover over the desert for minutes, rippling toward all horizons like water in a pool after a dragonfly touches down.

Even the sounds of the jet had vanished when Matthew pulled a large flaming splinter from the fire and lit a joint of Don Amerika's finest, tossing the splinter back into the flames when he was finished. It flared like the trail of a shooting star. "Tell me, Estevan. Tell me how the truth blinded you."

Estevan turned toward the sound of Matthew's voice. His withering body rustled inside his baggy plaid shirt and sunbleached overalls. "Okay, sonny. Just remember, you asked old Estevan. He didn't offer to tell you nothin' . . . ."

"Yeah, sure, sure . . . ." Matthew smiled in the firelight at how Estevan's empty eye sockets wrinkled up with mystery as he spoke. "Anyway, I like stories, Estevan." The way Estevan leered at him through the light, he'd swear there were eyes that could actually see sunk very deep inside those wrinkled sockets. A sudden breeze from the north chilled the air. Matthew laid on another piece of wood and wrapped Linda's serape tighter around his shoulders. Across the mesa, his gelding whinnied at the puma hissing at sounds in the night and the burro braying at the puma. "Lay it on me, old dude . . . ."

"Poor, blind Estevan . . ." the old prospector grunted again, wagging his shaggy white head.

30

"Somewhere around 1539, a Franciscan, Marcos de Niza, explored this territory in search of gold. With him he brought his trusted slave, Estevan. De Niza only desired more of what he already had more than enough of . . . gold . . . silver . . . precious stones. Living in the de Niza household, Estevan had not only taken the name of his master, but he also had learned what it was like to have wealth, to want for nothing. He, too, wanted wealth and all it could purchase. Estevan had become as greedy and impatient as his master.

"These treasure-mad pilgrims wandered across the bottom of what, now, is known as New Mexico, moving eastward toward what we call Texas. They had been out of food for a full day and had only one goatskin of water left dangling from the left side of the lead burro when they spotted the Black Mountains to the north of their trail. De Niza had heard stories of mountain dwellers whose cave floors were tiled with gold and silver.

After a full day of travel in the direction of the Black Mountains, they came upon a clear water pool at the base of the cliffs called El Morro. A group of Indians from the Big Sky pueblo, located near where the city of Acoma is today, were watering there. A desperate de Niza lied that they were peace ambassadors from a great king in a land across the great waters to the east who had come to the Indians' country to meet them in friendship. He offered the Big Sky pueblo three of their four remaining burros as tokens of peace.

"Now, the chief had often heard the drum messages in the night telling of hoards of olive and white people ravaging the lands far to the south for gold and silver and turquoise. They murdered like Apaches. They wore crosses of gold like the one de Niza wore on a matching gold chain around his neck. But, the chief was a fair-minded man. He refused to be swayed by the drums alone. Afterall, these men had not even violated the nearby sacred place--Keva. And, with only one burro remaining, they were truly at his mercy. So, the chief welcomed them and accepted their burros. De Niza and Estevan were accorded places of honor in his household once they had returned to the pueblo and passed around the locoweed-filled peace pipe carved from the thigh bone of an antelope."

"Would you like some?" Matthew interrupted.

"Some what?" Estevan's voice sounded shrill. "What?" His withered sockets seemed to twitch.

As he turned more directly toward Matthew, Estevan seemed to actually glare at him.

"Some locoweed? Top grade shit from one of the best underground connections in the country. Here, smell it burning?" Matthew shoved the joint under Estevan's drooping Romanesque nose. Coarse, white hairs bristled as the old man's nostrils flared.

"No. I can't smoke that stuff and tell my story straight." Estevan turned back to the fire. His nostrils curled back from their dusty bristles.

Matthew shrugged and sucked on the joint "Do your own thing, old dude. Do your own thing . . . ."

Estevan picked up his story, his voice a resonant monotone as if he had memorized the words of his tale without any inflections. "Now, the chief had a beautiful daughter. She was fifteen with a figure like twenty-one. Her hair was raven in color, and her eyes glistened more beautiful than gold in the morning sun when she would stroll to the washing well.

"The young princess was the only thing which drove the obsession for riches from Estevan's mind. Each morning he stalked her at a safe distance, dodging in and out of pueblo doorways, until she reached the well and began cleaning. First, the family's laundry. Then, herself. When she washed her body, she opened her hide dress by unstrapping the leather string which tied it down the front and dropped hand scoops of water from the stone bucket down her chalice-like breasts.

"One morning, during their second week in the pueblo, the princess was slinking down the dirt path when she suddenly turned around and began retracing her steps. Uncharacteristically, she wasn't carrying any laundry in her arms. Her move took Estevan by surprise. He was caught in the middle of the path. He dove for the nearest doorway. His heart pounded. He thought it would tear open his chest as he huddled in the doorway of the Medicine Man's pueblo.

"She must have seen him, he thought. She looked straight at him. As he peeked around the stone jamb, he saw her again walking down the path, dust puffing from behind her heels as she wiggled toward the washing well. It seemed to him that she was exaggerating her walk purposely, so he decided to follow and see what happened . . . . "

Estevan paused. He coughed and spit in the fire.

Matthew reached for the last log beside him and cradled it on the firecircle of rocks so that it straddled the flames. "You mean to tell me that old Estevan would not have followed the girl that morning if he hadn't thought she was walking in an exaggerated fashion? Come on, old dude. You can't be serious?"

Estevan's words continued to drone on through the fire and smoke as if Matthew had not spoken. But, Matthew was sure that he knew what would happen next. It, too, was as old as dreams of flight, like Estevan and "divide and conquer." As Estevan's monologue continued, Matthew's mind swirled through its own vortex.

There is a certain predictability in the human process. Estevan talks. He is talking as each moment of the continuing present is future, present, then past. The words, the results of his process, the sensation of mine. Are we no more than products of each others' minds? Matter shaped from the patterns of our thoughts? He wished Estevan

145

would skip the rest of the obvious stuff and move on to 'the truth', as he called it, whatever that was.

'The truth', indeed, Estevan! It can only be that there is no truth, and that can only be said with qualification, because we can't know anything truly enough to say we can or cannot know anything truly. The search for truth which the philosophers always lament is dying with them is just that, a search . . . as much for Eisenberg or Einstein as for Santayana or Sartre . . . the human process as closely as we can describe human process . . . life impetus.

What allows this process to exist as we understand it? Time. Time yields the results of process . . . . A knot on the new log popped, spraying red and blue sparks into the darkness above the fire. What was the old man saying, now?

"Poor Estevan tried to tell the chief that his daughter had tantalized him beyond belief. She had stripped herself at the well, pouring a full bucket of water over her shoulders and stroking her breasts, satin like the desert hills under the breaking dawn. She had opened her thighs in his direction and touched herself. She had known that he was watching. She invited him to enter her. He had been unable to control himself. It had been as if he had become someone else . . . someone completely obsessed with having her . . . .

"Estevan pleaded with the chief. The chief pretended that Estevan was a liar. Estevan pleaded with de Niza. De Niza pretended that Estevan was a stranger.

"With spike-like stones--maybe even some of the stones here in this fire circle--the medicine man gouged out his eyes as he lay spread-eagled on the sand, tied by wet leather tongs which would shrink as they dried in the sun and tear his arms and legs from their sockets. Through his pain, Estevan could hear them dancing around him and chanting for the sun to rise bright and hot. Suddenly, they were gone. He felt the sure death of the sun's heat caking the blood on his cheeks like a mask. Yet, he held one hope . . . that he would be born again from the princess's womb.

146

"According to the way the story has been passed down from father to son over the centuries, the way it was told to my father by his father and to me by my father, the first Estevan's bones are buried somewhere beneath these very rocks." He pointed a trembling hand toward the heat of the fire. "In fact, all of the Estevan's are buried here."

"Jesus!" Matthew gawked at the blackened stones which formed the firecircle, the altar, the grave marker. "Really?" He had recognized the formation as a fireplace, entertained the simile of an altar of smutted rocks reminding him of the old man's empty sockets. An altar built of holes. Matthew shivered. "I'm really sorry, Senor Estevan. I honestly didn't realize. I just didn't know . . . ." He tried to pull the serape which Linda had given him tighter around his shoulders, but it was as tight as he could make it already. "Jesus . . . ." He whistled softly, almost to himself. "Buried right here, huh?"

Estevan nodded at the fire.

"Well, at least you know where the bones are. They are right here on this mesa. My search has been for a friend. A friend whose death I fear that I may have been responsible for. Yet, I continually hear rumors about someone who looks just like him . . . who might be that friend. That he may, somehow, still be alive. So, I have not been able to stop looking. I have no mesa to go to where I know the bones of my friend are buried."

Estevan nodded. His head reminded Matthew of a lion's in the firelight and shadows.

31

"For four hundred and thirty years the first Estevan's dying hope has been a curse to my line. They were all born blind and doomed to be outcasts from their societies because of a common lust for gold which also seemed to be born in them. I was the first," he laughed bitterly, "to be born with eyes that could see. Ever since I can remember, my father told me that the curse of Estevan had finally lost its power . . . even though my mother did die at birth like all the others before me . . . ."

"Mine, too, Estevan. Mine, too . . . ." Matthew nodded his head. "Did you feel kind of responsible, somehow, once you knew about it?"

Estevan's creviced face turned toward Matthew again, his knurled fingers clasping Matthew's knees. "Sometimes, I still do."

"Yeah, I know what you mean, old dude. I know what you mean. It's a hard thing to get mellow about."

Estevan, turning back to the fire once more, fumbled in the air near the flames until he touched a stick of wood. Grasping it between his fingers, he poked at the fire, sending sparks into the night like meteors and comets shooting through galaxies.

"My father taught me what he called a new way. Gold was no longer the thing of value, he told me. Something was beginning to take its place. He lectured me about a fellow named Klaproth discovering it way back in seventeen eighty-nine, and how a whole bunch of fellows--physicses or something like that."

"Physicists," Matthew interjected.

"Physicists, then," Estevan spat at the fire. "They discovered this theory about it the same year as the four hundredth birthday of the Estevan curse. This was a sign, he said. But, he never said a sign of what . . . .

"So, he taught me how to use this new-fangled contraption that buzzes like a rattler when it spots this new gold . . . this uranium stuff. I can even do it without no eyes, you see." He gurgled in his throat like a warbler at his own little play on words.

"A Geiger counter! You have a Geiger counter?"

"Yeah." His voice was strained, accusing. "That's what it's called." His shoulders bunched under the blue-black plaid of his frayed flannel shirt. "How'd you know what I was talking about, sonny? Huh? You some kinda prospector coming in here to jump my claims?"

"No. Nothing like that, Estevan. Geiger counters are just something I learned about in college or in the Army or somewhere along the way, you know?" He scuffed his boots in the red dust. "Do you think I could, maybe borrow it later on, just for an hour or so? I want to make a few readings over at the bomb test site. Ground Zero. You know where I'm talking about?"

The moon was fading over project Manhattan. "Yes, I know." Estevan's voice seemed to gargle a sardonic laugh as he waved the flaming stick he held in his left hand in the direction of the Southwest as if he could see it. "Ground Zero." He flung the stick into the fire and dropped his head into his hands. A snarl of pain tore from his craggy lips. "That's where my story ends . . . ."

"Odd," Matthew muttered, more to himself than to Estevan. "That's where my story begins . . . ."

"Yes. I know . . . ." The old prospector, then, continued with his story, again, almost as if the interlude of their dialogue had never taken place.

"Every year my father brought me to this place overlooking that desert out there to commemorate the end of the curse with a sacrifice. We always came here the day before the ancient Estevan supposedly died. We would make camp. The following morning we would burn a blood offering on this very fireplace . . . always the eyes . . . of a prairie dog . . . of a lizard . . . of an owl or a hawk . . . . My father used to say that it reminded him of the story of Abraham and Isaac in the Bible. I would always answer that

149

I hoped that God would never ask him to sacrifice me. He would laugh from real deep in his flabby belly. 'No, son," he'd say. 'You don't have to worry none about that. You're blessed by God, son, not cursed like the rest of us.'

"Of course, I believed him. After all, he was my father. I was his son. Why would he lie to me?" Estevan sighed as if he were about to cry. The puma's pads thumped in the dust in the darkness as she glided to his side, it seemed, to comfort him.

"All of a sudden, I was twenty-one and left alone to hoist my father's corpse over his burro, strap it down with hemp rope, and make the three-day trek from out base camp to this place. Rattlesnake bit him. Damn slimy creature bit him right in the jugular vein."

32

Morning was beginning to edge into the sky in streaks of gray and amber on the eastern horizon. The sun would be coming up soon. Matthew coughed. He poked at the edges of the fire with his boot toe to try and hide his impatience. "So, Estevan, what is this 'the truth' you've been going on about? What is 'the truth', really?"

Estevan sucked in a deep breath to damn the sobs flowing through his words. "A few weeks later, I led an expedition of white men into an old burial grounds less than a day's ride from here. They was looking for uranium, and I knew where there was a bonanza! I was cocky at twenty-one, blessed by God, you see. And, I never thought that burial grounds would still be considered sacred around here . . . in the United States of America . . . not anymore. Not even my own family's burial grounds . . . ." His lips curled into something between a sneer and a grin.

Matthew sat forward and started to respond, to say, again, how sorry he was, but Estevan held his hands up palms away from his body and toward Matthew. "No need, sonny. No need."

Matthew sat back, and Estevan continued.

"But, the old Sky tribe did. They captured me after the white men made camp and bedded down for the night. They brought me here almost a full day's ride. They knew that this was my tribe's burial ground. They tied me down with wet leather tongs, just like their ancestors had tied down my ancestor more than four hundred years before. According to our family legends, at this very spot.

"I knew I was as good as dead, but I was real puzzled when the Medicine Man didn't poke out my eyes with stone needles or something. I had expected that. They just vanished with the first morning breezes across the desert. I was left alone on this mesa with the rising sun already getting hotter by the minute. When I turned my head I could see a small herd of antelope grazing on the other mesa which was covered with scrub brush and prairie grass rather than dust like this one. Wings of vultures beat overhead.

"It seemed like hours later when I heard the explosion ripping through the morning light. The concussions shook the mesa under me. I jerked my head southwest for a look at what was causing the loudest explosion I'd ever heard in all my life.

"A glowing jade cloud mushroomed into the rose sky. The antelope herd stampeded. Existence smeared like paint on glass. My eyes dribbled from their sockets. In a matter of seconds, the antelope vanished and I was blind."

Matthew placed his arm around Estevan's slumped shoulders. The old prospector's chest heaved. "It's okay, old dude. It's okay . . . ." For an instant, in the fire light and shadows, Estevan's face seemed to reshape itself . . . . Was it Jason he saw lurking somewhere in the depths of the old prospector's face?

"Blind. Blind. Poor, blind Estevan!" He twined vine-like fingers around the boy's arms that embraced him, holding him fast. "I'm the only one what knows. The only one what saw!" He released Matthew with his left hand and stroked the puma's head as she sprawled in the shadows by his left leg. "No-cat, here, saved my life, though. She discovered me about noon. I was better than half dead. My lips were cracking open, sort of raw like. My eyes had dried on my cheeks. The drying tongs had stretched my arms and legs to near their limits but hadn't, yet, ripped them from their sockets. No-cat, the evil fiend, thought that she'd found herself some easy eatin', didn't ya girl?"

Estevan scruffed the dome of the puma's head with his knurly fingers. "But she felt sorry for me, I guess. She must've been able, somehow, to sense my helplessness like she might one of her own cubs, because after she scared the shit out of me growling and purring and hissing and sniffing around my body, she began chewing through the tongs one by one rather than chewing on me.

152

"And, she's watched out for me ever since. She's been my eyes, my protector. Haven't you, girl?" He again ruffled the scaly fur on No-cat's head. "Helps me hunt out my uranium. I swear she can smell the stuff. Uranium, that is." She purred. "She's about half dead now, herself, poor old No-cat."

Matthew wagged his head, poked at smutted stones with his boot toe. "I've got news for you, Senor Estevan. It's no longer uranium that matters. It's information. Information is the new gold. The new uranium . . . . Let No-cat sniff around in the desert for that . . . ."

"No!" Estevan's bowed Psalter lips sneered, eyeless gouges above them blooming like abysses in the growing morning roseness. "I'm the only one what knows the truth!" He leaped to his feet, fumbling for Matthew's arms again. "I'm the only one what saw it!"

GODZO.

Matthew instinctively reflexed backwards, yanked his left arm free of the closing vice of Estevan's groping fingers, combat crawled from the fading glow of the fire toward his bedroll near the east ledge. He could see the Winchester's silver barrel beginning to take on a luster in the dawn light.

GODZO.

A low, slow wind drifted from the southwest over dryrotting outhouses, disintergrating concrete bunkers, crystalized sand, and rattling chain link fences carrying the memory northeastward like the fragrance of enchilladas.

GODZO.

Estevan stalked the sound of the boy . . . the scent of the boy. He could smell him like the puma could smell uranium. "I'm the only one what knows it. Poor, blind Estevan." He howled like a pack leader getting wind of prey.

GODZO.

"Your eyes, sonny! They've got to go on the fire!" The prospector's gravel voice became Yosemite Falls crashing onto the mesa. "You don't need them to find your friend.

153

He's dead just like you are, boy. Just like all of you are!"
Maniacal laughter shredded his lips. He raised his hands
like a falcon's talons above his mangy head. "Now, that's
'the truth!'"

Matthew's hair bristled on his neck.

Estevan's hulk blotted out the glowing coals of the fire
as he lunged after the sound of the boy's reacting body. He
could hear him scrambling on his stomach back to where he
had been before. The old man stumbled in the direction of
Matthew's bedroll.

GODZO.

Finally, Matthew felt the cool metal of the Winchester
between his clawing fingers. Forgetting that the rifle was
loaded, he levered a round into the chamber, expending an
unused round into the red dust, now chocolate in the violet
dawn . . . and letting Estevan know exactly where he was
located.

GODZO.

Estevan leaped for the sound of the lever, landing on his
belly atop Matthew's blanket. "Your eyes, boy! I need your
eyes!"

Matthew rolled to his left, again into the browning dust,
chalk in his mouth, like a barium milkshake.

GODZO.

"Got to have your eyes!" Estevan flailed stick arms and
legs tangled in the army blanket like that dying meadowlark
had flailed its wings under the weight of Jason's aldrin snow.
Each had been crazed by a different poison.

GODZO.

Matthew set himself in a prone position. He pressed the
linseed-oiled stock against his cheek and shoulder, took a
deep breath, released his breath evenly. He did not hold his
breath at all. He simply ceased breathing. He squeezed the
trigger.

GODZO.

The sound of the rifle shot seemed to echo off every mesa. Blood spurted from a volcano in Estevan's chest. Matthew's gelding whistled, reared his hobbled hooves.

GODZO.

Jackass squalled.

GODZO.

No-cat never moved or made a sound. She just peered through the morning air in the direction of Estevan sprawled spread eagle in the chocolate dust near the eastern edge of the mesa.

GODZO.

Matthew crawled toward the old prospector. His rifle dragged behind through the luminescent rust of years that covered the mesa.

GODZO.

The earth had been warm when Matthew began. Now, in his hands, shards of Estevan family grave markers still gouged at cool mesa dirt as he carved out a hole in the charred, fire-softened soil underneath the dead campfire. While he dug with sharp stones that could be the very ones that gouged out the eyes of the first Estevan, he could not avoid thoughts of another more hastily dug grave in The Hole near his father's house. The hole where he had buried the meadowlark his father had murdered with his poison snow last Christmas. Now, he was burying the old prospector he, himself, had killed. Both father and son claimed self-defense.

Was this, then, a beginning or an ending? he wondered as he rolled Estevan's corpse into the hole. While he shoveled dirt with his hands to cover the body, he realized that he was burying much more than Estevan in this shallow grave.

Matthew broke camp in the funereal silence of the desert dawn. He unhobbled and saddled the gelding. Before mounting, he stood beside the grave, staring at the charred stones, now, marking a new burial in the Estevan family burial grounds. The final Estevan.

He suddenly was struck by the fact that he had not spoken any words over the old man. He had left no written epitaph. He reached for his saddlebags. The gelding whinnied. Its left flank twitched as he opened the leather bag. He pulled out his pen and the Rolling Stone. Its pages constituted the only available paper other than his diary. And, he was already writing on the backs of those pages. He thumbed through the tabloid rock 'n roll paper until he spotted a Sam Goody's ad with lots of available white space. He began to scribble in the white spaces. When he finished writing, he tore the ad from the paper and replaced the Rolling Stone in his saddlebags.

He had written the words. Now, how did he preserve them? Against the slow onslaught of the desert? Searching his saddlebags again, he located the plastic bag which had previously held his birthday eggs. The plastic was clean and dry. He folded the page from the Rolling Stone with his words scribbled on it to fit the baggie, pushed as much air out as he could, then sucked out the rest. He sealed the words safely inside. That would protect the words from the sun and the winds. Safer than it had been for the meadowlark or for Estevan . . . or for Ward . . . . Safer than it would ever be for him or for those whom he called "brother" and "sister."

Matthew slipped the words-in-a-plastic-bag underneath the stones he had used to dig the new grave. Here, old Estevan. The stones will protect the words against predators.

"It's no Beowolf, but it relates the essence of our encounter here on the mesa in the desert overlooking GODZO. 'The truth', if you will, of our night and morning together.

"How did we put it, old prospector? This was where your story ended and my story began? That was what we agreed, wasn't it?" Matthew mounted the bay. "Adios, Senor Estevan. Adios! I'm really sorry that it had to end this way. I really, really am . . . . Adios . . . . Adios . . . . Adios . . . ."

He cantered the gelding into the purples and pinks showering the desert from the morning sky as the sun began to rise above the still-gray eastern edge of the earth. He turned back in his saddle just once. The monument of charred stones appeared as a lumpy black hole in the mesa. "Adios, Ward. Mi amigo. Adios . . . . Adios . . . . Adios . . . ."

Once Matthew's horse had negotiated the descent from the mesa table to the desert floor, he reined the quarter horse in. Up to that point, the gelding had known the best way. Now, he had to take the reins. Hell, the livery place had a deposit for the value of the horse anyway. He'd call them from Denver and let them know that he had absconded with their prize bay gelding. What were they going to do? Hang him in the square for horse stealing?

Matthew clicked his tongue and pulled lightly on the left rein. The horse turned one hundred and eighty degrees. He touched his heels to the mount's haunches. They galloped northwest past the words he had scribbled on the Sam Goody's ad that seemed to be emblazoned upon the wine dark western horizon like a second sun.

> *Here lie the ashes of Estevan*
> *Blinded by the bomb,*
> *Crazed by the sun.*
> *Murdered by my gun,*
> *Rest with your uranium,*
> *Blind, mad, dead, last Estevan.*

As they headed toward Denver, toward Emmy Lou, he did not look behind him again, so he did not notice the silhouettes of two riders on the eastern horizon. They seemed to be riding hard toward the twin mesas.

To contact Timothy Brannan or order copies of his other works: *Into the Elephant Grass: A Viet-Nam Fable, TEACH, Manhattan Spiritual, Adventures in Another Paradise*, and *'74: A Basketball Story* please shop, write, or e-mail as follows:

www.amazon.com

Gemini Publishing
2828 N. Atlantic Avenue, Apt. 502
Daytona Beach, Florida 32118

tbrannan@cfl.rr.com

2347799

Made in the USA